THE
DREAMER
AND THE
BELIEVER

ANTHONY DUNN

PAGE PUBLISHING, INC.
New York, NY

First originally published by Page Publishing, Inc. 2017

ISBN 978-1-64082-100-2 (Paperback)
ISBN 978-1-64082-101-9 (Digital)

Printed in the United States of America

CONTENTS

CHAPTER 1

And Justice for All

"All, rise! The Honorable Judge Adams presiding."

Judge Martin J. Adams appeared in the courtroom wearing the typical long black robe and his complementary intimidating expression. He ascended the few steps to his bench.

"You may be seated," said the bailiff.

Dressed in a forty-dollar suit that may have fit him before he discovered Krispy Kreme, my attorney, Rob Zinski, grunted in my direction, "Hope for the best, kid, but prepare for the worst. I could only do so much."

I guess hoping is all you have when you can't afford an attorney.

I reached out for the paper cup of water and noticed that my hand was trembling. The analog wall clock clicked each dreadful second.

"I have reviewed your case, Mr. Taylor. You have been found guilty of drug trafficking to an undercover officer. Given the amount you had on you, state law allows for quite a stiff penalty. I could put you away for a long time. However, since this is your first offense, and from what your attorney has said, I am going to apply the minimum sentence of five years in the Oaksville Penitentiary."

"Thank you," was all I could choke out.

"Mr. Taylor, when you are serving these five years, I want you to reflect on your life and how to better yourself. I don't think you're a terrible person, but I want to be a lesson for bettering your life. Do I make myself clear?"

"Yes, Your Honor."

His gavel descended, and the bailiff escorted me from the room.

My name is David Taylor, inmate number 1147. I was born in Cleveland, Ohio, on June 3, 1976. Adopted from an orphanage at the age of five, I found myself in trouble numerous times with life at a young age. When I was growing up, I never had any real discipline; my motto was that I would do whatever I wanted, whenever I wanted. My foster parents were the worst parents I had ever known. I wore dirty clothes every day with holes in them. Some days I couldn't shower, and when I did, it was only for a few minutes. All they cared about was the money they got from the state government, so I would come in and out of the house whenever I pleased.

I would roam the streets at night stirring up all kinds of mischief. It started with tagging at the age of thirteen, then went to burglary. Luckily, I never got caught or shot dead, but one thing led to another, and before I knew it, I was hustling drugs for money. I started to build quite a small reputation when I was seventeen. Many people don't know this, but a teaspoon, a hot flame, and over-the-counter drugs can fix up quite the addicting batch. Like nicotine entering the body, it can be very pleasurable. I was constantly on the move from one abandoned building to the next. Sneaking around like the Grinch, only this Grinch wasn't after presents.

The night was a breeding ground for criminals and dopeheads in Cleveland. I had to be careful and watch out for some of the black gangs. They were not too fond of a white boy hustling and taking all the profit. If you were caught on their turf, you might as well put a gun in your mouth and pull the trigger. On late nights between 1:00 AM and 3:00 AM, you would hear gunshots ring out in the distance. Nobody would scream or make a noise; everyone around was used to the violence. Sometimes, if girls didn't have enough money to cover the drugs, I would make them go out of their comfort zone. I was a sex addict, and if they were really cute and really wanted to get high, I would bend them over in a dark alley and stick it where the sun didn't shine. You would be amazed at what people would do just to get high. Figured by now, you would have considered me a tooth decay to society. In my mind, I thought I had everything going for me. Women, drugs, money, what more could a young teen ask for? But my ego got bigger and bigger, swelling up like the body's reaction to a bad injury, and the person I was becoming wasn't tolerable.

That all came to a crashing halt when I got busted selling to an undercover officer. One of the whores I slept with got busted and ratted me out to the authorities. So they set up a sting operation and put me away for five years at Oaksville Penitentiary. This is where my story begins and how my life started out on the wrong path to destruction but quickly changed for the better. Well, I say that for now.

I was delivered to Oaksville Penitentiary on July 21, 1994, along with twelve other convicted felons in a fortified school bus. As I was sitting near a window, I could see my reflection in the glass. My hair was short and thin along with a clean shave. Staring beyond the trees at the sun as it rose in the distance. Armed guards with pistols stood at each end of the bus watching our every move.

When I arrived at the penitentiary, I knew that I was going to be the last man on the totem pole. This was home to some of Ohio's nastiest criminals. Most of them were in here for murder, rape, and drug trafficking like me. As I slowly stepped off the bus, a chill ran down my spine. I could see all the other prisoners staring at me through the barbwire fence, like I was an all-you-can-eat buffet.

They were hanging on the fence eyeballing each and every one of us. It was almost like they were placing bets as to who would belong to who. Shackled and escorted in a single-file line, they took us into the prison. This place was nothing but concrete walls and bars.

We walked down a narrow hall and into a large briefing room.

"OK, inmates, take your clothes off!" The guards shouted as they made us strip off all our clothes and change into orange jumpsuits that had a barcode number on the back. We were identified by the number on our suits; my number was 1147. The guards then made us line up side by side. A tall, stalky white man with a suit and tie entered the room. He had a clean military-style haircut and meant business as he walked by each and every one. Staring at us like a rabid beast ready to kill, smelling us as if we reeked of garbage.

Then, he stepped back, raised his voice and spoke firmly, "My name is Sergeant Dean, and I am the warden here at Oaksville Penitentiary. You are considered a piece of shit to society, and that's why you are here. I want you to know that your life now belongs to me in this place, and I can make it your worst nightmare. Some of you are going to be here for a long time, some of you will have a chance to rehabilitate and get your freedom back. You will follow orders at all times! I will leave the dice in your hands, and you will decide how rough you want your life to be, but I do not recommend the hard way. Do I make myself clear, men?"

"Yes, sir!" we all yelled.

"OK then, welcome to Oaksville, you're dismissed."

The security guards took us to our cells. As I was being escorted down the hall, some of the other inmates behind bars started whistling at me and barking like dogs in heat. "Look at this guys a new kid on the block!" Another one yelled, "Hey, boy, I can't wait to get my hands on you and make you my bitch!"

He reached out and grabbed my arm, pulling me toward the cage as I was walking by. Smiling at me with rotten teeth and blowing me kisses, the guard pulled out his baton and hit it against the cage.

"Back off, Billy, and shut the fuck up, or I will throw you back in solitary!" he screamed.

This forced him to let go of me. As we continued down the hall, the guard whispered in my direction, "If there is one piece of advice I'm going to give you, kid, is that you try to avoid the ones like Billy. He likes to rape men, especially the new guys, and he seems to take a liking to you already, so be careful."

Hearing that made me sweat a little. The thought of a man wanting my butt hole wasn't the most pleasant thing. As I took a few more steps, the guard stuck his baton out against my chest. "Stop right here, 1147."

"Open cell number 62!" he yelled.

The gate started to slide open.

"Here you go, inmate, enjoy your new home for the next five years, and by the way, welcome to hell."

The best thing I could do was ignore him. I stepped into the cell, and then he yelled again, "Close cell number 62!"

The cell door closed behind me, and there I stood staring around a 9 × 12 concrete cell with a bunk bed, toilet, and small metal bench that had a stool attached by a swivel arm so you could read or write on.

The walls had all different types of languages etched into it. A stainless-steel toilet was attached to the back wall next to the bottom bunk facing out toward the cell door. The mattresses looked like they were pulled out of a dumpster in the bad part of town. There was a bald older man lying down on the bottom bunk reading a book. He looked to be in his midforties with a medium build and some tattoos on his arms. The most recognizable one was a cross with the name Angie tattooed on his forearm. It looked like he had been seasoned here for a while.

He lowered his book just enough to where you could see his dark green eyes staring at me. "Top bunk is yours, boy, no ifs and/or buts," he spoke.

I didn't know what to say at first, so I climbed up the bunk and lay there until someone came and told us it was time for lunch.

A guard called for us all to step out of our cell and walk in a single-file line to the mess hall. The mess hall was this huge open lobby with long rows of tables and chairs where the inmates sat. At the far end, they had the buffet table where the chefs stood behind. Once I got there, I grabbed a lunch tray and stood in line. As I was working my way down, the chef scooped this pile of what looked like canned dog food out of his pan and dumped it on my tray. I looked up at him with disgust on my face. He smiled at me with his two teeth and double chin, "Enjoy some of Oaksville's finest."

I grabbed the tray and just walked away. I didn't know where to sit. I noticed as I looked around the room that the blacks sat with the blacks and whites sat with the whites. Same went for the Mexicans. So I decided to go sit near the white section to avoid any complications. Lots of faces were staring at me. They knew I was one of the new guys. The food wasn't that bad, but as I was eating, another inmate walked up and sat across from me.

A little old man with no teeth and a very bad comb-over. He leaned over the table and said, "Hey, man, what you in for?"

"Drug trafficking, what's it to you?" I replied.

"Sorry, I forgot to introduce myself. My name is Robby, and I'm the go-to guy here at Oaksville. If you need anything like cigarettes, booze, etc., I am the man for the job. That's how I survive in this hellhole. This is your first time, isn't it?"

"Yes, it is, and look, man, I really appreciate the offers, but I just want to be left alone and do my time."

"I understand, David, but that's not going to work for you in this place. You have to make friends, or you will end up in a coffin, or better yet, you will become someone's bitch."

"How the hell you know my name, and why are you telling me all this?" I asked.

"Take a good look around, bub. I've been here so long that I've seen what they do and how they operate. Rape, murder, stabbings, and since you're a new guy, you're a sitting duck."

I said with confidence, "Thanks, but I can take care of myself."

I started to stand up to put my tray away, "You're so fucked," he whispered.

"What did you say?" as I turned back around.

"I said you're so fucked!" He started laughing, showing his rotten teeth as I turned and walked away. He had one of the most evil laughs I've ever heard. I shrugged it off and acted like that's not going to happen. Once lunch was over, we went back to our cells.

Throughout the day, they would release some of the inmates to go outside and exercise. When I was in the yard, they had some exercise activities for us. They had a basketball hoop and some weight-lifting equipment. It had a big open field section for running. A massive double barbwire fence surrounding the whole entire place with four guard towers in place. In between the barbwire fence were very sharp rocks. So if you managed to jump the first fence, you would probably shatter your ankles on the rocks before getting to the second fence. Each guard in the tower had a high-powered rifle with a scope.

The same way they acted in the mess hall was the same way out here. All the races stuck together, so my instinct told me to go hang near the whites. When I was walking over toward them, I bumped into a small, skinny white guy named Eddie Lee, and he filled me in with everything I needed to know about the yard and how to avoid any problems. The yard was the easiest way for anyone to get attacked or killed. He said that two years ago, there was a massive gang attack that happened right where I was standing, which left ten wounded and nine dead. That explained why the guards had rifles in the towers. I really appreciated everything he told me, and I kinda shadowed around the white guys the rest of the time I was out there. Luckily, everything was calm in the yard that day.

As my first day was winding down to an end, there was still no communication between my cellmate and I. It was very awkward because he kept to himself and stayed very quiet. I wasn't going to bother him. He looked like a ticking time bomb just waiting to go off.

CHAPTER 2

Too Late Too Late

The next day I was awakened by a loud siren going off and inmates yelling at the top of their lungs. I immediately jumped up out of my bed and tried to look outside the cell. There were officers running down the hall in full riot gear. More screaming and yelling were coming from down the hall. I couldn't see what was going on, but from what I could gather, it sounded like an inmate was going crazy. I pushed my face up against the bars, but I still couldn't see well. Then, I heard a guard yell, "Put it down, I said put the fuck down, or this is going to end very bad for you!"

Other inmates were gathering in their cells to see what was going on. Then, all I could hear was the guards rushing with clubs swinging. Everyone was talking and yelling, so it made it even harder to hear. About five minutes later, I saw an inmate in handcuffs being dragged down the hall with blood all over him. He was yelling, "It was time for him to pay for what he did, and now it's up to God to decide!"

The paramedic team came running down the hall, and soon after that, I saw the victim on a stretcher completely covered in blood. It looked like a scene out of a horror movie. Blood was dripping off the stretcher and on to the floor. My hands started to shake as reality started to sink in. This man was stabbed with a prison-made shank thirty-seven times in the chest. The guards were telling everyone to settle down and ordered us to back away from our cell doors. Never in my life had I seen a dead body before; there was so much blood, it made my stomach start to turn. I had to look away.

I soon realized why they called this place hell on earth. They ended up locking down our side of the prison to clean up and do their investigating. Some think it was an assassination called upon by some high-ranking gang member. Come to find out, it wasn't an assassination. The man who was killed was in here for raping and killing a six-year-old girl. Inmates didn't tolerate people who harm children. If you touch a child, you might as well kill yourself before you come here.

The entire time this was going on, my cellmate just sat in his bed reading his books. He was very quiet during all this and didn't say a word. I imagined this was nothing new to him. A few nights went by, and I was having a lot of trouble trying to sleep. All I could see in my head was blood and death. In the distance, I could hear some men screaming in pain as they were being raped. The agonizing screams would lightly echo through the prison at night. What would possess a man to want to have sex with another man? I guess if you haven't been with a woman in twenty years, you would bang anything. I knew that if my cellmate tried that, we would fight to death.

Then the following night, I was lying in bed just staring at the ceiling. I'd been here less than a week and was getting cabin fever real bad. So I decided to lean over my bunk and grab one of his books. He kept three or four books lying around next to his bunk. As I was reaching down, I was only inches away from getting a book when a hand grabbed me, yanking me off the top bunk. I fell hard landing on the side of my shoulder. He jumped on my back and put me in a chokehold.

As I was gasping for air, "What the hell is wrong with you? Are you trying to get yourself killed!" he yelled.

"I'm sorry, I just wanted to read something, please don't kill me," was all I choked out.

After about sixty seconds, he finally let go of me, and I crawled into the corner and turned around gasping heavily for air. The man said, "Do you have a death wish, kid?"

"No, man, I don't, I didn't mean to cause any problems."

It took a few seconds for the situation to calm down, and then he continued, "Sorry, I might have overreacted a little bit, but you can't be doing shit like that in here. I had a very bad experience with my last cellmate, so I am always on edge."

He reached his hand out, "Name's John."

I shook his hand and held my throat with the other replying, "My name is David, David Taylor. Nice to finally get a chance to speak with you, John, and is it OK if I ask you what happened between you and your old cellmate?"

"Yeah, he decided one night I was going to be his Marilyn Monroe, and let me tell you, it didn't go very well. He was ten times bigger than me, so I had to put up one hell of a fight. Luckily, I was able to hit him in the throat hard enough to put him down."

"What the hell is wrong with this place and everyone wanting to rape each other?"

John chuckled and said, "Not everyone is like that, it's just some of these men have been here for many years, and they tend to lose it upstairs. Whacking off only gets them so far, plus I had long hair back then, and that was a mistake. Hallucinations will happen, and that uncontrollable urge will make a man act on it, but luckily, you have a buzz cut, so you should be fine. However, if you wanted to borrow a book, buddy, all you had to do was ask."

"Yeah, that was stupid of me to do that. Growing up, I always did what I wanted to do."

"You can't do that here, they will own your ass. You're lucky it was me and not one of the other inmates because you would have been in a body bag. Just like what you witnessed the other day."

"That was some of the scariest shit I have ever seen. Hey, how long have you been here?" I replied.

"I've been here for nineteen years, and I'm here for life, buddy. How about you?"

"I am here for five years for drug trafficking. I thought I was hard core out on the streets, but I was wrong. What did you do to get locked up?"

"Look, kid, I don't know you that well, so I'm not going to talk to you about it," replying with anger.

"OK, sorry to ask."

"Well, I don't know about you, but it's late, and I am going back to bed, but I want that book back when you are done."

"No problem, man, have a good night."

It was nice knowing that I finally got to carry out a decent conversation with John.

I climbed back up my bunk and started to read a book called *From Success to Failure,* which was kinda ironic, but it sounded good. The book was based around a man who had it all as a stockbroker and lost everything. He went from living in a penthouse to living on the streets. I read a couple chapters, and then I decided to call it a night. I was one of those guys who falls asleep reading after a couple chapters.

The next day, tension started to rise as I was out in the yard minding my own business. I was sitting on a bleacher stand when a gang of four black thugs started heading in my direction. They were big dudes looking for trouble. When they approached me, I did the best I could to ignore them, but it didn't work.

"Well, guys, looks like we got ourselves another dumb white cracker. You know you're in our territory, bitch?" one guy said.

I replied with a smart-ass comment, "Oh, I'm sorry, I thought this was property of Oaksville Penitentiary and not some wannabe gangbangers." This wasn't the time to show weakness so I had to be strong.

Then, the leader of the group who had a huge scar from above his right eye that ran all the way down to his cheekbone, "What the fuck did you just say to me?" He reached out and grabbed me by my collar and lifted me out of my seat. The other three gathered around ready to do whatever he ordered. We were eye to eye, and I'm not going to lie I thought I was going to die.

My heart was beating through my chest, and then I heard, "Stop what you're doing, and let go of him!"

I thought it was a security guard, but out of the corner of my eye, I saw John standing there with a couple of big white dudes.

Looking to his left he said to John, "Tell me why this cracker is in our territory?"

"This isn't your territory, now let go of him, there is no need for violence."

"Fuck you, John, I don't think so! I am going to make an example out of him!" he shouted.

One of the white guys standing well over six feet and about 250 lbs. of pure muscle got in front of John. "Listen here, nigger, I am going to count to three, and then I will break all four of your necks."

"One... two...," Before the count of three, he let go of me.

He looked me dead in the eye again and whispered, "You're lucky this time, bitch, but you haven't seen the last of me. Next time, your friends won't be able to help you."

He said to his brothers, "Come on, guys, let's go." They began to walk away.

Staggering over I cried out, "Oh damn, thank you, guys, for what you did. I need a new pair of underwear after that."

The big white guy said back to me, "You really need to watch what you do out here, newbie. You could have been killed today." "Your absolutely right and thank you again."

As the day went on, I spent some more time talking to John out in the yard. We sat on a bench staring into the yard. John said, "I see you met Tyron."

"I'm assuming he is well known around here."

"Yeah, you are very lucky, David, he is very dangerous, and do your best to avoid him. If it wasn't for Cue Ball, I wouldn't have been able to save you." "So that's his name, well make sure he knows I am very thankful."

As our conversation continued, his side of the story started to come out. "I'm not a big fan of violence, David. I have been around it for years now, and I try to coach some of them who still have a chance at freedom. I know I'm never getting out of here, so I want to help some of the inmates as much as I can. Some learn and some don't."

"Why help them if you don't even know them?" I asked.

"Life can be a beautiful thing, and to watch people keep making the same mistakes drives me nuts. There are many guys in here who look to me as a father figure in their life, and I have helped many of them over the years. I have also watched many of them cut their lives short."

In that moment, I knew that John didn't belong here, and I had to be real with him.

"You know, John, something tells me that you should have never ended up in this hell. So cut the bullshit and tell me what happened to you before all this?"

With a look of sadness on his face as he put his head down and kicked some dirt around.

He went on to explain. "I had a family and a son before all of this. My parents didn't have much money growing up, but my father always told me money wasn't everything. I didn't have much education, and so I skipped out on going to college. When I was older, I worked at the steel factory doing everything I could to supply for my family. I had a stay-at-home wife with a newborn son. Everything was going good for a couple of years until the factory started laying people off.

"I was on that list, and that's when I struggled trying to find another job that would support my family. Bills started piling up along with stress. I didn't have a lot of skills besides working in the factory, so I only knew that path. One day I got a phone call for another job interview in this distribution center. I landed the job, and I was so excited to tell my wife when I got home. When I walked through the front door, I saw a small trail of blood leading into the living room, and I could hear my son crying. I stepped into the living room, and there I stood in shock as I dropped my keys. I saw my wife lying dead on the floor, and my son was in his playpen crying for mommy."

I put my hand over my mouth and cried out, "Oh my god! What happened?"

"She killed herself by cutting her own throat. My wife, like most of us, had issues, but I never thought that she was capable of killing herself, but I was wrong. She was on antidepressant drugs, and she needed more help, but it was too late. When the cops showed up, they immediately arrested me and took my son away. I told them everything and how I was innocent, but I should have never removed the knife from her hands. My prints were all over it, and that's all the jury needed before they tossed me away like a piece of trash. I told the truth and nothing but the truth, but my testimony meant nothing to these people. I was lucky enough not to receive the death penalty. I tell you, the system is so screwed up it makes me sick. I'm not the only innocent man that has been locked up. If the damn jurors would quit going off on emotion and more of what the evidence is, many people would be found not guilty."

I had this look of shock on my face as he told me all this. John was an innocent man just rotting away in prison till he dies. I asked him if he knows anything about his son, and he said no. I told him I was sorry for both his losses.

"Anyway, David, enough about me, tell me a little about yourself and why you're here."

I went on to explain, "I was adopted from an orphanage, and so I never had the chance to meet my real parents. From what I was told, my father was a pilot, and he and my mother were flying on a business trip when the plane's engine stalled, and they both were killed. I was so little that I don't remember. I was a wild child growing up though, in and out of the house running with the wrong crowd.

"For the most part, I wasn't too bad, but the real trouble started when I was in my teens. I started not caring about education, so I would skip school whenever I felt like it. My buddies and I would smoke dope and play games. I got into drug hustling because the money was good and so was the girls. I didn't have any morals, the way I ran my life, I didn't think I would have made it this far. The girl I was banging on the side got busted with my drugs, and so she ratted me out.

"The damn cops set up a sting operation, and I got busted for selling to an undercover officer."

After I explained everything in detail, John just took a breath and said, "You know, David, it's not too late for you to turn your life around. You're not a bad kid, just made some mistakes and ran with the wrong crowd. If I were you, take my advice, when you get out of here, find out what it is that you enjoy besides that and chase your dream. 'Cause you will either end up back here or six feet under. I have seen it happen over and over a hundred times. Remember you are in control of your destiny."

John then stood up and started to head back inside. At the moment, I looked through the fence out into the sunset. The sun was orange, and the sky was clear. John made a lot of sense when he spoke. The guards then yelled at the rest of us saying it was time to go back inside.

CHAPTER 3

Lover Man

I was six months in when one of my worst nightmares was about to come true. I began the day by doing some simple workout exercises like push-ups and sit-ups and then I would write in my journal. I would write almost every day in this journal to remind me of why I will never come back here. It was peaceful, and it kept me occupied. The morning seemed very quiet, and none of the inmates were getting rowdy. The worst part about prison was the shower arrangements. It was one big open concrete room with showerheads all along the walls.

All the water would drain into the center of the room. I hated standing naked in a room with a bunch of dudes, but I had no other choice. On this particular day, I became the target again. Everyone was minding their own business and slowly making their way out of the shower room. I was the last one there and was just about finished when I turned my head and saw Tyron and his bros walk in the room.

They looked right at me. I turned my head whispering, "Oh, God, no," hoping they didn't recognize me, but they did.

Tyron spoke out loudly, "Well, would you look at what we got here, boys? It's the smart-ass punk who got lucky out in the yard a while back. I told you I would come for you."

"Stay the hell away from me!" I screamed loudly.

"Looks like your buddy John and Cue Ball aren't here to help you."

"What do you want from me?"

There was an awkward silence, and then he said, "Oh, I think you know." As they came at me fast, I threw as many punches as I could. I knocked one down, then shoved another away, but I was out numbered.

As fists were flying, I tried to scream for help, "Help! Somebody help me!"

I was in one big scuffle, and then a fist came in from the side, knocking me unconscious. I fell hard, hitting my head on the concrete floor. Bouncing off the floor like a basketball. I had blood running all down the side of my face.

When I started to come back to my senses, I found myself on my belly, and my vision was coming in and out. They had me held down as I tried to yell for help again, but my speech was mumbled. No one was around, not even a mouse could hear my cries. Two of them were kneeling down on my arms, and the other one had me by the back of my neck. The third guy was cheering them on, "That's right, boys, we going to teach this motherfucker a lesson."

I started tearing up as Tyron leaned over and whispered in my ear, "No one can help you now, boy, the more you lie still, the quicker it will be."

I was breathing heavily in a puddle of water mixed with my blood.

Then, I felt a tight pressure in my rear end. I bit down on my lip in agony and screamed. My veins were about to explode out of my head as I was trying to resist. There was not a damn thing I could do to stop it. As if it couldn't get any worse, he got off me and said, "OK, boys, it's your turn now." They took turns performing sexual acts on me. All four of them raped me in the shower that day.

These were some of the sickest-minded people in prison. When they were finished, they left the room, and I remained lying there bleeding. Torn and in massive pain with blood running all down my backside. Nothing but the sound of water dripping out of the showerhead in the distance.

Crying like I never cried before. My friends and I used to joke about not dropping the soap in the shower when we were kids. I now know what it really means. My pride was completely stripped away.

A security guard found me shortly after, and I was taken to the infirmary. I felt so ashamed and worthless because they immediately knew what happened. The doctor came in to examine me and take some X-rays. After the results came back, he said I would be fine, just very sore for a couple days plus a little spotting, but that's normal. All I could think about at the time was killing myself. I was so traumatized and didn't know how to cope. I spent a day in the infirmary and then I was sent back into hell.

When I got back to my cell, I was limping real bad, and John was just lying in his bunk. He looked at me, and he knew what happened. "You OK, David?"

"No, man, I'm not OK. I'm fucked up in the head right now." I sat against the wall on the floor from across his bunk and tried not to cry or show any more weakness.

"I know what happened to you, and you know that if you need anything, just let me know."

I couldn't hold it in anymore, and then I burst into tears. I covered my eyes with both my hands and said, "They raped me, John, they fucking raped me. I can't take this anymore. I am going to kill them one by one."

John leaned out of his bunk and put his hand on my left shoulder. "David, listen to me, you don't want to do that. You will never be able to step outside these walls ever again. I know what you're going through isn't easy, and it will take time to heal, but remember what happens in here stays in here, and when you leave this place, try your best not to take it with you. I will see that this doesn't happen again, and I give you my word. I know you can get through this."

I replied while wiping my tears, "Thanks, you're like my only friend here. I feel so weak and pathetic. I used to think I was untouchable, but boy, was I wrong."

"You have to stop thinking about it right now, OK? First things first, you need some rest, so hop up in your bed and try to take it easy. If there is anything you need, and I mean anything, just ask me."

For the next few days, I just lay in my bunk acting like a zombie. I couldn't sleep, and if I did, I had nightmares about it. I barely went outside nor did I want to take another shower.

John would talk to me every night about random stuff to help take my mind off it. He was like a therapist, and I couldn't thank him enough for what he had done for me. I spent most of my nights self-reflecting on my life.

Writing in my journal was a big help, but it was time for me to really get serious and do what's right for me. On a quiet night, John suggested that I start reading the Bible. He said to me as we were lying in our bunks, "David, have you ever read the Bible?"

"No, man, I don't believe in that. Sorry, I hope I don't offend you. I don't know what to believe or not."

"You know I used to say the same thing until I came here."

Staring at the ceiling, listening to what he had to say.

"I used to lie for many nights blaming him for why I got locked up. Thinking to myself what in the hell did I do to deserve this. I finally picked up the Bible and started reading it. It took some time, but eventually, I started to realize that the devil is real, and evil does exist. The devil tempts us every day, and deep down inside, I believed he is the reason why my wife is gone. The devil walks among some of the men in this very prison. The murders, stabbings, and rapes are just part of his game. God once said, 'Do not envy the violent, and do not choose any of their ways.' When a man sees the light and starts to believe, that's when his or her life changes for the better. It made me want to help people and become a better person. I have done things in my past that I regret and hope I don't go to hell.

"We all have sinned, but sins can be forgiven. So that's why I suggest you give it a read sometime. It's totally up to you, David."

I replied, "If the church is supposed to represent good, then why are priests molesting boys?"

John sighed, "OK, David, think about it as I question you. What is the most powerful opposition to the church?"

"Well, I would have to say evil."

"Right, now think about a powerful castle for a second. It is one of the most powerful castles on earth, and its king represents good over evil. So let's say, you're evil and want to take down the castle. It's obvious you can't take them head-on, and so how would you try to bring down the castle?"

I paused for a second and tried to answer the best I could, "I guess I would have to find a way inside and bring it down from within."

"Good, now we're getting somewhere. You're using your head and thinking outside the box. This is exactly what is happening to the church. There were child molesters who became priests and infiltrated the church and attacked it from within. It's not just the church though, it happens all over the world and especially here in the United States. Communists would love to destroy this country, and they are here undercover. You keep thinking outside the box, David, you will do just fine."

I took John's advice and started reading the Bible, not because he said so, but because I wanted to. I want to better my life, and within a few weeks, I started to get my sanity back. I manned up to what happened and moved on. I would read a little from the Bible every night and continue to write in my journal. I started believing in a better path, and writing major events in my journal would take me back and help me reflect more on my life and why I wanted to change.

One day I learned from a couple inmates chatting next to us that if you maintain good behavior, the prison will reward you by letting you do more activities. I had another couple of months to go before they would evaluate me. It ended up taking a full year before the warden finally did my evaluation. Within that year, I managed to survive with no further injuries or attacks of any sort, but then that day came again.

I would help mop the floors in the evening to get more brownie points and maybe shave some time off if that was possible. Right before my evaluation, I had another incident happen one evening when I was putting the cleaning supplies away. I was inside this small, narrow closet full of cleaning supplies. I was just straightening everything up when I heard the closet door shut. I had my back facing the door. I quickly turned around, and there I saw Tyron. I dropped the mop broom and stared him right in the eyes.

The closet wasn't very big, just a couple of shelves on each side. He said in a deep voice, "I'm back for more, sweetie pie, and there is nowhere to hide."

My heart was pumping fast along with sweat rolling down my face. John told me this would never happen, but Tyron planned it and planned it good. I had to strategize my attack because that was the only way I was leaving this closet alive. Tyron came at me fast. My first instinct was to kick him in the balls. Once I got my right leg up, he grabbed it and flipped me on to my backside. I tried crawling back as fast as I could, but I was running out of room. Cleaning supplies were falling off the shelves as he jumped on top of me and grabbed me by the throat. His hands were massive, and he squeezed my windpipe as hard as he could. I only had a few seconds to react, and what I am about to tell you might save your life one day. I let go with my right hand and reached in between his legs. I grabbed him by the balls, and I squeezed and twisted as hard as I could. Twisting and yanking as hard as I could, it caused him to let go of my throat. Tyron screamed and cried out in pain. I had him dead to rights as his eyes rolled into the back of his head, and he immediately passed out. He fell backward and hit his head on the concrete floor. I stood up over top of him as he lay there like a dead fish. Nobody was around, so I kicked him in the head a few times while he was down and closed the closet door behind me. That was the last time anyone ever tried to mess with me. I imagine that Tyron's buddies found out, and they just left me alone.

I didn't say a word to anyone, and I passed my evaluation with flying colors. I was sent to the warden's office to receive the news. I walked in and saw Sergeant Dean was sitting behind his fancy oak desk. He had a very nice office, a big window behind him where he could look out into the yard. A couple bookshelves on each side of the wall along with a ceiling fan above his desk. He tilted his reading glasses down and looked up at me as he was reading my paperwork. "Inmate 1147, you have been on the right path to rehabilitation and have had good behavior for quite some time now. You haven't been causing any problems here at Oaksville, and since I am in a good mood, I will be kind. I know you had an incident in the shower room a while back, and since you're showing mental stability, you will be rewarded. You can go up to three hours a day in Section F of the prison any time you want."

"What is Section F?" I asked.

"*F* stands for fun, and yes, I know it sounds ridiculous, but I didn't name it. There will be all kinds of activities for you to do with other inmates. However, you only have one chance not to fuck up, or you will be never allowed back in there. Do I make myself clear?"

"Yes, sir, I understand, and thank you."

"OK, good, now get the hell out of here, I have work to do."

A guard took me to this section of the prison. It was a secret room that I never knew existed unless you were on good behavior. When I walked in, I saw about twenty to thirty inmates doing all kinds of fun stuff. I saw a Ping- Pong table along with a poker table. Also saw a couple of inmates shooting pool. There were a couple of small tables in the corner with board games on it. They also had a big screen with a movie called *Braveheart* being played.

It felt nice to be here, but there was one thing that caught my attention in the corner of the room. It was an acoustic guitar with a music stand beside it. I walked over to check it out. I always wanted to learn how to play when I was a little kid, but my foster parents wouldn't let me. As I approached it, it said Fender on the headstock and had six strings. I didn't know hardly anything about guitars, but I really wanted to learn. I picked up the guitar and sat it on my lap. I opened the book that was on the music stand. It was going to teach me everything about learning how to play and the theory of music. The introduction talked a lot about the fundamentals and basic chords that are commonly played throughout music. The first chord I tried to learn was a G chord. My fingers didn't want to go into position. My hand felt handicapped, but they talked about how your hand has to adjust to what you're trying to do. The book said a lot of beginners get frustrated and quit. I had to hang in there, and I eventually started getting the swing of things. Strumming that chord was even tougher 'cause my hand-eye coordination was way off. The book also talked about taking your time and perfecting it, so I wouldn't develop any bad habits. Once I learned the G chord, the next chord I tried to learn was a C chord. After about an hour, I was getting a little frustrated, and my fingertips were hurting bad. It mentioned that you will have a little pain until you build up your calluses. I had to stop there because I was running out of time plus my fingertips were killing me. I wrote in my journal that night about it, and the next day I woke up excited to go back and learn more.

John and I spoke that morning about it. "So did you enjoy your time in Section F?"

"How did you know I was in there yesterday?" I asked.

"I used to be allowed in there all the time until I screwed up."

I said in a joking matter, "Let me guess, you got caught whacking off to a hot chick in one of those movies."

"No, you perverted ass, I got into a very intense poker game and lost my cool. I had a flush, and this guy beat me with a straight flush, so I threw the table across the room and got thrown out." We both laughed at the situation.

"So I take it you like music, David? Well, maybe when you get really good, you could entertain us. The prisoners could use it, and so could I. Maybe it would keep them from raping and killing each other."

"I am a long way from that stage, but I will try my best to learn as much as I can while I'm here. What kind of music do you like, John?"

"Oh, I like rock 'n' roll. Some of my favorite artists were Elvis, the Beatles, and the Rolling Stones. Let me tell you I did some jamming back in my day."

"I never listened to a whole lot of music growing up. I was always out on the run doing dumb shit, and look where it got me." I said.

"Hey, you can't keep beating yourself up. Just take from it and learn like I said before."

"Thanks, and anything new with you this morning?"

"No, just the usual, waiting here till I die."

"When I get out of here, I will see if I can talk to some people and let them know your story."

He laughed and said, "Don't waste your time, buddy. Trust me, you won't get far. Just go and enjoy your life and never look back. I just better not see your ass back here, or I will kick your ass."

"Hell, no, I am never coming back here and that's a promise."

"So you're saying you wouldn't even come back to visit a friend?"

"Of course, I would come back to visit. You knew what I meant by that."

"Oh, I was just playing, and that's great. If you're very serious about learning music, David, you need to listen to some of those artists, and that will help you with inspiration."

"How am I going to be able to do that?" I replied.

John looked out the cell door to make sure no one was around, and then he lowered his voice and said, "I got a good relationship with one of the guards, and I will see if he will sneak in a cassette player for you."

"You can do that for me!" I shouted.

"Hush, keep your voice down, and yes, I am sure I could pull that off for you, but you have to do something for me in return."

I immediately said, "Yes, of course, what do you want?"

"I want you to learn a song called 'Angie' by the Rolling Stones. My wife's name was Angie, and that was our song we danced to at our wedding. If you could do that for me, then we got a deal."

I reached out and shook his hand and made a deal.

CHAPTER 4

Bad Seed

About a week later, a guard by the name of Darrell walked up to our cell. Darrell leaned towards the bars and whispered, "Psst, hey come here quick."

I headed over there as quick as I could. "Yes, sir, what do you need?"

"Don't ask questions. Just stick your hand out quick."

As I stuck my hand through the cage, he quickly placed a Sony Walkman cassette player with earplugs in my hand. I pulled my hand back and said, "Man, thank you so much for this."

He whispered to me, "The only reason I did this is because of John. You didn't get this from me, and this is the only conversation we are going to have. Do I make myself clear?"

"Yes, sir, and thank you." I turned around and climbed back into my bunk. John wasn't here at the time all this went down, but he did make it happen. I opened the cassette player and out popped a tape that said "rock and roll mix one" on it. Other guards started to walk by, so I quickly put the cassette tape back into the player and placed it under my pillow. The only time I was going to be able to listen to it would be at night. When John arrived back to the cell, I told him that his buddy stopped by and delivered the goods. He said the same thing to me that the guard did. We had to keep this a secret, or we would never see the light of day.

That night I pulled it out from under my pillow. I put the earbuds in and pressed play. I lay there all night rocking out to some amazing tunes. I wasn't sure who the artists were, so I asked John who was on the tape. He said most of the bands on there were AC/DC, Kiss, Rolling Stones, Pink Floyd, Led Zeppelin, and the Beatles. He had that song Angie on it, and I fell in love with the acoustic sound. I continued to listen to it over and over for the next couple of weeks. I was beginning to excel on the guitar very quickly. I would spend at least a total of six hours listening to music and playing guitar. Only three of those hours were on the guitar. I was catching on fast and started getting some of the other inmates' attention when I was playing. They would stop what they were doing and listen to me play. They would cheer me on after each simple song I learned from the book. I started getting ballsy by listening to the Walkman in the middle of the day instead of at night. It was becoming my new addiction.

My addiction came to a stop about six months later. I was lying in my bed reading a book while John was below resting. Then, I heard what sounded like guards searching through cells. I jumped up and immediately went down and woke John up. I shook him as I whispered, "Oh no, John, they are searching through everyone's cell. What am I going to do about the Walkman?"

John was quick to respond, "Quick! Just jam it in your pillow-case and pretend you're sleeping. Try to remain calm and don't act nervous."

I quickly jumped back up and jammed it in the stuffing on my pillow. Then, three guards approached our cell. One guard shouted through the cage, "OK, you two, out of your bunks and up against the wall now!"

I tried acting like I was sleeping, but that didn't matter. We had no other choice but to do what they said. John and I got up against the wall and put our hands where they could see them. The guards started searching our entire cell, and lo and behold, they found my Walkman. He shook the hell out of the pillow, and the Walkman fell out hitting the ground.

"What the fuck is that? Is that what I think it is? Well, I'll be damned someone's got some explaining to do. You two stay where you are, and someone get me the warden."

A few minutes went by, and Sergeant Dean made his way down the hall to our cell. Once he got there, he said, "What seems to be the problem here?"

The guard lifted his hand up to show him the Walkman.

"Which one of you is responsible for this?"

We both were quiet for a second, and then he said, "If one of you don't tell me, I will lock both of you in solitary for six months."

I started to open my mouth, but right as I did, John spoke up saying, "Mine, Sergeant, the Walkman is mine."

"You managed to smuggle something into my prison? Guards, see to it this man gets punished for what he did, and then afterward, throw him in solitary for three months."

Sergeant Dean then turned his back and started to walk away. I went to speak out, but John told me to shut my mouth. The guards then pulled out their batons and began beating John right in front of me. He was yelling in pain, and then they started dragging him down the hall. I stood there in anger ready to attack them, but I knew what would happen. That was a brave thing he did for me, and I don't know what else they had in mind for him. I was all alone now with no Walkman nor a cellmate. I listened to that mixtape probably over a thousand times, so it wasn't a huge loss but John was.

Expressing my anger and hatred through it as I continued every day cranking away on the guitar. I was constantly thinking about John wondering if he was OK. Wasn't long after that I was minding my own business while entertaining a couple of inmates. A guard by the name of Rex came up to me and said, "You, buddy with the guitar, stop what you're doing."

I was playing some Johnny Cash for these couple of guys. So I stopped, and the inmates got a little pissed at the guard.

"Sorry, sir, if I was being too loud, I will stop."

"No, that's not it. The warden wants to see you, so come with me," Rex said.

I put the guitar down and followed him to the warden's office. I asked Rex if this was going to be good or bad, but he didn't answer me. We were slowly approaching his office, and I started getting sweaty. Sergeant Dean was a pretty intimidating guy. I'm sure he knows how to make a grown man cry. As I walked through the door, I could see the back of Sergeant Dean's head. He was sitting at his very expensive oak desk with his chair facing the other way. Smoke was floating to the ceiling as you could hear him puffing on a cigar. He rotated the chair around and said, "One one four seven, I've been getting reports about your music playing in Section F. The guards have been saying you are quite the entertainer with that guitar."

"Thanks, I just really enjoy playing, and the other inmates in there seem to enjoy it too."

"Let's cut the bullshit. I know the Walkman wasn't for John. It was for you. Do I look stupid to you, do I?"

"No, sir, you don't."

"Yeah, I didn't think so. Take a seat, I want to show you something."

I sat in his chair directly across from him. The sergeant then turned this picture frame around that was sitting on his desk. It was a picture of him with some guy holding a guitar. I didn't know the guy holding the guitar, so I played it off stupid. I said, "Is that who I think it is?"

"Yep, that's me with Bob Seger. He was a good friend of mine back in the day. I used to help lug his gear around before he got famous. I went into the military right before he blew up, and so that was the last time I talked to him. I am a big music lover, and so I got to thinking. I am going to make you an offer. I want you to play a small show for all the inmates. They could use some entertainment, and I will provide a small PA system for you. Can you sing?"

"Yes, I can, but I'm not the greatest at it yet."

"That's good enough for me," he said.

This was a chance for me to make a deal back. "I will do it, but I would like something in return."

Sergeant Dean asked me what I wanted, and I said, "I want John released from solitary, and I will learn some of Bob Seger's tunes for you."

He leaned back his chair as if I caught his attention. "OK, I am listening."

"I also need the Walkman back, so I can perfect the songs more by listening to them."

Sergeant looked me right in the eye and took a hit of his cigar, "Deal." Then he looked over to the guard and said, "Rex, go release John from solitary, and give him back the Walkman. You better not disappoint me, David."

CHAPTER 5

Hero of the Day

When I was taken back to my cell, it was only a few minutes later until John arrived. He had a huge smiling grin on his face as we walked through the cell door. He said, "I don't know what, I don't know how, but what the hell kind of deal did you make with the warden?"

"I have to put on a show for all the inmates here soon. I found out that the warden is a big fan and friend of Bob Seger. So I told him I will learn a couple of his songs for him if he would let you out of solitary, and so he did. I also told him I needed the Walkman back with a new cassette mix, so I can study the songs."

John started to chuckle and said, "I don't know how to get the warden to kiss your ass but I appreciate you getting me out of that place. Many men lose their minds in solitary. Did you remember to put 'Angie' on that list?"

"Of course, I did, we had a deal, and I wasn't going to break it."

John was superstoked and said, "Way to wheel and deal plus earning yourself some brownie points with the warden. I am proud of you, buddy, and looks like you got some work to do."

Over the next couple of weeks, I learned everything, song and lyric for the show. With only a couple days left to go, I was getting very nervous. If I go up on that stage and choke, it will be the death of me. This is my first time ever performing, and it's in front of the scariest tattooed criminals in the country. The day finally came, and it was time for the big show. A couple of guards came and got me and took me to the mess hall where we all eat lunch. I could hear hundreds of inmates talking out loud behind the door. My hands started shaking uncontrollably. Sweat started rolling down my face as I walked into the mess hall. All the inmates were still being loud and annoying. I saw the PA system and the guitar leaning against a black stool. I approached the stool and picked up the guitar. I adjusted the microphone to my comfort zone. Slowly easing my ass down on to the seat.

I mumbled into the microphone, "Um, hello, my name is David, and I am here to play you guys some tunes. So sit back and enjoy."

The inmates clearly were ignoring me, and then I looked up and saw Sergeant Dean standing in the second-floor balcony. He had the look of anger on his face. I got my fingers into position and started to pick the first notes to the song "Angie." I made a promise to John, and as soon as I did that, I saw John's face light up with joy. John started rocking his head back and forth, signaling me to keep going. He believed in me, and then the inmates started to settle down as I closed my eyes and started to sing the first verse.

"Angie, Angie, when will those clouds all disappear." I was terrified to open my eyes back up. When I finally opened them, I saw all the other inmates turning their heads toward me. Then the whole mess hall suddenly got quiet. All eyes and attention were on me now. My heart was racing at a thousand miles per hour. I thought I was going to have a heart attack and die because all the inmates were looking at each other like what in the hell is this. Then I froze up and stopped playing. I got real still. The entire mess hall was so quiet; you could hear a pin drop.

An inmate stood up in the distance. Closing my eyes again; afraid he was going to yell something. What he did next changed the entire outcome. He continued singing the next part of the song out loud by himself. He sang, "Angie, where will it lead us from here?" Then, out of nowhere, the entire mess hall erupted, and everyone joined in. "With no loving in our souls and no money in our coats. You can't say we're satisfied!"

I came back in with the guitar, and they were grabbing on to each other, rocking back and forth, singing their hearts out. It was almost like they were too embarrassed to sing along with me until that man did what most prisoners wouldn't do in front of each other. After I finished the song, they all began to cheer and clap. My heart rate then began to decline. I was starting to have some fun, and so were they. I started to play "Sweet Home Alabama" for my second song, and their singing just got louder and louder. I looked back up to the balcony, and the look on Sergeant Dean's face was priceless. I went on to play a couple of Bob Seger songs, and before I knew it, I was out of songs. Time flies when you are having fun. All the inmates were overjoyed with the thought of live entertainment. I gained a lot of respect from the other inmates. From there on out, I had this feeling that this is why I was sent to prison.

When that night was coming to an end, John and I had a real close conversation as we were lying in our bunks. John said, "David, that was an awesome thing you did for all of us, and thank you for playing 'Angie' for me. I know if my wife was alive, she would have loved to hear you play it."

"You're welcome, John, you know it won't be long before I get released from here. I really want to pursue music once I get out of here."

He followed up with, "I know, man, it's going to suck, I kinda enjoy having you as a cellmate. If I were you, I would take that guitar and do something great with your life. Or kill someone so you can stay here forever."

We started laughing. Then he continued, "You know I'm kidding. I want to see you become successful and follow your heart. Be an inspiration to people and teach them the right way. Once you forget about the past, you will do great. Many people don't get a second chance at life. The world can be just as dangerous out there as in here."

"I'm nervous because I will have nobody but myself. I don't even know where to go or what to do once I'm out."

"You will be just fine, you survived in here for this long. You're a smart kid, and I have faith in you. Just follow your heart, and it will show you the way."

I leaned over my bunk and said, "What did you want to be before all this?"

What he said then almost brought a tear to my eye.

"I wanted to be a good father to my son and give him the best life I could. I hope he is out there doing something great with his life. The sad part is that I will never know. Now I know you're tired, so get some rest, rock star, you earned it."

"Thanks, John, and have a good night." After that, I just lay back in my bunk and stared at the ceiling. I had a lot of trouble sleeping that night because in my heart I'm the only one who knows he is an innocent man. How many other men out there are innocent and locked up?

The next morning, Rex came and told me the warden would like to see me again. So I went back to his office, but this time, what he said was a total shocker. He said as I entered, "Well, that was one hell of a show you put on for those boys. The attitudes around the prison this morning have been good, and since you have shown great signs of rehabilitation, I am releasing you from Oaksville Penitentiary. As of today, you are no longer being called Inmate 1147. You are a free man, Mr. Taylor."

I stood there in shock for a few seconds and then said, "Um, how is that going to fly with Judge Adams? Legally, I thought you can't do that?"

"Yes, I can't release you for good behavior, but have you ever heard of compassionate release?"

"No, sir, I haven't," I replied.

He then said, "It's a process by which inmates in criminal justice systems may be eligible for immediate early release on grounds of particularly extraordinary or compelling circumstances which could not reasonably have been foreseen by the court at the time of sentencing. This can only be mandated by the courts or by internal corrections authorities. So your incident in the shower room is enough for them not to ask questions."

"Sorry to ask, but don't you have to be at least sixty years old or something like that?" I asked.

He took a big puff of his cigar and said, "If you don't stop asking me questions, then you will serve out your full sentence. All I will say is that your life is in danger, and your health is at risk. I have a lot of authority and respect from everyone, and so I can bend the rules a little. Plus the prison is getting overcrowded, and so I strongly suggest you get your shit and get out before I change my mind. We didn't have this conversation as well."

I have never seen the warden act like this before. He was a dickhead most days, but for some reason, he had a change of heart. Rex took me back to my cell to grab some of my things. I said goodbye to John as he stood up and shook my hand with confidence.

"Good luck, my friend, and may your dreams come true. I know you're going to go far in life. One other thing, never say goodbye it's always see you later. To me when you say goodbye means forever my friend."

"Thank you for everything, and I couldn't have done it if it wasn't for you. I will come back someday and visit."

It was sad to have to leave him, but he knew that this is what's best for me. As I was walking out the front door, I heard the warden yell my name in the distance. I stopped and turned around as he said, "Aren't you forgetting something?"

"No, I think I got everything."

"No, you forgot something that has six strings," he said.

I just had this small grin on my face as I saw the warden holding the guitar. He was going to give me that guitar that belonged to the prison. As I reached out to grab it, he whispered to me, "You better rock the world because if you end up back here, I will personally fuck you up."

I looked him dead in the eye and said, "Yes, sir."

I took the guitar, and out the door I went.

CHAPTER 6

Wherever I May Roam

Once that gate opened, I stepped through it and paused for a second, closing my eyes. The sky was blue, and the sun was beating on my face. The calm, breezy wind was blowing my long brown hair. Freedom was the best feeling in the world. This was it for me, a chance to start over and begin a new and better life. I spent four and a half years in Oaksville and was not looking to ever return. A yellow taxicab was waiting for me just outside the gate. I opened the door and then slowly turned around. I stared at the front of the prison for a second and then loaded up the guitar and got in. The taxi driver said to me, "Hey, man, where you need to go?"

"Take me to Cleveland please, that's my hometown."

It was about a two-hour drive back home. When I arrived, nothing had changed for the better. The streets were filled with trash, and more buildings were left abandoned. I didn't live exactly in downtown, more in a run-down suburb just outside Cleveland. After being dropped off, I didn't have a clue where to go or what to do. I couldn't go back to my foster parents' place because I was over twenty-one. I realized that I had to move on with my life. I had no transportation, so I started train hopping from one town to the next. It wasn't the quickest way to get around, and it was cheap.

I spent two full days drifting on the trains until I came across this little town called Chesapeake. It was located near the Ohio River. I don't know what it was, but something in my heart told me to hop off, and so I did. It was just after midnight. It was a warm summer night, and the stars were out. Thunder was roaring in the distance soon after getting off, so I knew rain was moving in. With nowhere to go, I decided to nestle up under a bridge next to some railroad tracks. It had a concrete overpass for cars. Graffiti was sprayed all over the underpass; the ground was hard and full of rocks. I found a soft patch of grass, and that's where I would rest. I could hear the raindrops at first, and then it just poured down hard. At least in prison I had a bed and a roof over my head. I used my book bag as a pillow and stayed the night under this bridge. I had to find a way to get some money. I could have gone back to selling drugs, but I tried to avoid that path again.

The next morning, I scouted the town looking for work. I stopped into stores and restaurants but was immediately turned away. I had long hair and probably smelled like a bum, considering I hadn't showered since I got out of prison. I came across this gas station that had a sign out front saying "Now Hiring." When I was standing in line waiting to speak to the clerk, an older man in front of me accidentally dropped a fifty-dollar bill without noticing. I looked around real quick, then picked up the bill. In my mind, I was fighting between good and evil on whether to keep it or give it back. I needed the money badly, and the other part of me was saying give it back. The man then stepped to the front counter. He started to panic as he realized he was missing money. I was back and forth in my head. Then I tapped him on the right shoulder, "Sir, I believe this is yours."

He turned around and said, "Oh, thank you so much, you're a lifesaver." I gave the money back to him out of the goodness of my heart. The man was very appreciative as he left. I spoke to the clerk about getting an application. He reached under his counter and handed me one. As I was leaving the store, that same man was waiting for me outside. He approached me and said, "You know, not too many people would have done what you did in there. Most people would have took off with it, so I want you to have this money because I think you could use it more than me."

My face lit up with joy, "Thank you, sir, I really appreciate it, and what makes you think that?"

He replied, "No problem, buddy, I saw your guitar, and I assumed that you weren't a book salesman but a struggling musician. I know what it's like to be a struggling musician. I was like you when I was younger. I chased a dream for about ten years, so I wish you the best of luck." I shook his hand and thanked him one more time before we departed.

Now that I had a little bit of money, I could survive for about a week. I bought some cheap food and showered at the local truck stop. At this truck stop, I managed to buy a cheap razor to clean up my face. I also bought a hat and a hair tie so I could keep my hair knotted up and tucked away under my hat if I wanted to. Got a couple new shirts and a decent pair of pants. My shorts were looking pretty disgusting, so I just threw them away. I kept my old ratty pair of Chuck Taylors because that's all I had for shoes. Later that day, I was wandering around town and stumbled across this little place called Shelly's Diner. It was starting to get dark, and I was getting hungry. This diner was very small and looked like it could only fit about fifty people. When I walked in, I saw a black bar top with red padded stools lined up along the front. Behind it were a couple of older waitresses serving coffee to some folks. I looked to my left and saw red padded booths with white tables. One of the waitresses behind the counter shouted, "Hi, welcome to Shelly's, please have a seat wherever you like."

I picked out a red booth in the corner by the window and gazed out as the sun started to set. I placed my guitar and book bag on the opposite side of the booth. The place was no bigger than a Waffle House. Then a cute waitress about 5'10" with beautiful long brunette hair walked out from the kitchen and approached me. Her name tag said Erica, "Hey, hun, what can I get you?" she said.

"Oh, I will take a water and then could I get some warm soup? What's your soup of the day?"

"Our soup of the day is chicken noodle."

"Yeah, that sounds good, I will take that."

"You, OK, darling? You look like you've had a rough day."

"Oh, I'm fine, it's just been a lot longer than a day."

She started to giggle and told me she understood. Which she doesn't have a clue, but it's whatever. She then went and got me my drink and soup. When she came back to the table, she asked me, "Hey, you must be going to open jam tonight."

"What makes you say that?"

"Your guitar, silly."

I had this dumb look on my face because I didn't have a clue about what she was saying, so I had to tell her the truth. "I am new to town, and I don't know much of anything."

She said, "Oh, hun, that's OK. The place is called Dino's Bar 'n' Grill. They just built it about a year ago. They got decent food along with live entertainment."

"Well, thank you for telling me this. So are they having open jam tonight?"

"Yeah, tonight at nine thirty, and it's only about a mile up the street."

I didn't have anything better else to do, so after I finished up, I grabbed the guitar, and off I went. This guitar so far must have been my good-luck charm. I got fifty dollars earlier plus what the waitress just said.

I walked all the way to a place called Dino's Bar 'n' Grill. You couldn't miss it. It was a big brick building that had big neon letters lighting the sign up. As I walked through the double doors, you could see a stage all the way in the back. They had a bar with the kitchen attached from behind off to the left side of the building along with some tables and chairs for eating. On the opposite side, they had some pool tables and dart games. They had a big standing section right in front of the stage. You had to walk down a few steps to get to that section. They also had more seating in the balcony that wrapped around from above. This place was definitely done upright.

I walked up to a table where they were having sign-ups. There were about ten people who signed up, so I put my name on the list and told the gentleman at the table that I was new to this. "Hey, dude, it's all good. Just have fun," the gentleman said.

It was cool because they had a drum kit and amps already set up for anyone to play on. I went back up and sat at the bar and ordered a drink. Then, a couple of older folks got up on stage to kick things off. They played for about fifteen minutes, and they were very talented at playing all different styles. It didn't take long before my name was called. I grabbed my acoustic and hopped up on the stage. The drummer and bass player stayed on the stage. They asked me if I wanted to play alone or jam with them. I told them, "Let's jam, guys, and see how it goes."

This was my first time playing with a live drummer and bassist. The drummer said, "What song would you like to jam, buddy?"

I stood there for a second. "Um, how about 'Blue on Black' by Kenny Wayne Shepherd?"

"Yeah, good choice." The drummer did a four-count, and off we went. So far we were thirty seconds in, and everything was sounding tight. Then, out of nowhere, a man in his early twenties with long black hair and tattoos approached the front of the stage. He had a torn-up leather vest on over his Guns N' Roses T-shirt. His jeans looked like it just went through a shredder. He looked at me dead in the eye and was trying to say something to me, but I couldn't hear, so I stopped the song. The drummer and bassist did the same.

"You gentleman are missing something for this song," the guy said while pointing his fingers at himself.

"What is that, my man?"

"A badass lead singer, dude!" he shouted.

The drummer then said to me, "Hey, man, Sebastian is a good singer, and he wants to know if he can come up and sing the song."

I looked back and forth between both of them and said, "I am new to this, guys, and I don't care if you guys don't."

Sebastian shouted, "Got ourselves a new guy in town, well, buddy, we're all brothers here at Dino's, so let me kick some ass with you so you can feel right at home."

He then jumped on the stage and grabbed the microphone. He then said to the crowd, "Hey, everybody, we got ourselves a new guy in town. What's your name, partner?"

He put his hand over the mic and leaned over to me as I said, "My name is David Taylor."

Then, he yelled back into the microphone, "His name is David Taylor! So give him a big Dino's rock 'n' roll welcome."

I was embarrassed as hell as everyone clapped for me. Then the four-count was initiated, and off we went again. Sebastian came in strong with his vocals, "Hey, blue on black, tears on a river, push on a shove. It don't mean much. Joker on jack, match on a fire, cold on ice, a dead man's touch, whisper on a scream doesn't change a thing. Don't bring you back, oh yeah, blue on black."

This guy sounded amazing behind that microphone. Everyone in the room was looking in our direction. Some people were tapping their foot and singing along. After we played a couple more songs together, my time was up. I was sweating harder than a pervert masturbating in a sauna. Once I was finished, Sebastian invited me over to the bar to have a drink.

"Bartender, I need two Budweisers please. So, man, you are pretty damn good with that acoustic guitar."

"Thanks, man, I have been playing every day for the last four years, so it's been paying off."

"Sorry, I forgot to properly introduce myself, my name is Sebastian Rose. I sing lead around here for fun, plus it keeps me near the music."

We shook hands as I replied, "My name is David Taylor, I am kind of new around here, so I thought I would swing in and check this place out. Thanks for the beer by the way and giving me a shout-out even though you embarrassed the hell out of me."

"No worries, brother. Hey, let me ask you, have you ever played electric guitar, or are you straight acoustic only?"

"No, I would love to play electric, but this is all I had and learned on."

"You seem like a cool dude, how about I make you a deal?"

"What do you have in mind?" I replied.

"If you show up to next week's open jam and play a couple songs with me, I will let you jam on my electric, OK?"

"Oh, really, what kind of guitar is it?"

"It's a Gibson Les Paul, and it's very expensive, but I want to hear you play it."

I didn't know much about the guitar manufacturers because of prison, so I played dumb. "Hell, yeah, man, that would be awesome. I will be here next week for sure."

Sebastian seemed like a really cool guy even though at first he struck me as an egotistical prick, but I was wrong.

Sebastian then said, "Hey, David, I got to go, but you enjoy that beer, and I will see you next Thursday at 9:30 PM."

"Hey, no problem, I will be here."

Sebastian then bolted out the door, and shortly after that, the place started to close. I grabbed my book bag and guitar and headed back out on to the street. I stayed the night under the bridge again.

CHAPTER 7

Welcome Home

Sometime around 3:00 AM, I heard footsteps and two guys talking nearby. I didn't think much about it until I felt my book bag get pulled out from underneath me. I immediately opened my eyes and jumped up. There were two thugs with dark clothes running along the tracks with my guitar and book bag. I chased after them yelling, "Give it back! Give it back, you fucking assholes!"

I ran as fast as I could. My heart was pounding, and my adrenaline was pumping. One of the men that had my book bag tripped on the railroad tracks. I caught him, and we started wrestling and throwing punches.

"You fucking prick, I'm going to kill you!" I yelled.

His other buddy was long gone out of sight, and it was just me and him. I had him by the throat with one hand and hitting him with my other. It was a white guy with a nasty beard and a couple of teardrop tattoos on his face. He also had tattoos all up and down his neck. This guy was the complete definition of trailer trash. My guess is that they both were high as a kite on something. Everything was happening so fast that I didn't see him grab a rock nearby and bust me in the side of the face. I immediately let go and rolled off him, and it damn near knocked me out. He got up and took off running where his buddy went. I lay there for a sec, and my vision came back. I reached over and grabbed my book bag, but my guitar was long gone. My hand was bloody, as I got to my knees and started to cry. I felt like nothing was ever going to go right for me. I nestled back up under the bridge and waited until morning.

The next morning came, and I was more than sad; I was a walking zombie. I walked into town to the local pawnshops and asked them if anyone was trying to sell them a Fender acoustic. Every one of them said no, and they would be on the lookout if anything were to come up. As I was walking downtown, something caught the corner of my eye. It was a little music store that looked like a hole in the wall called Dick's Music Store. I crossed the street to check it out and ask him if he knew anything. As I walked in, a little bell rang from above to notify the shop someone was coming in. Once I was in, I saw all kinds of cool stuff. He had amps for sale that were lined up along each side of the wall, and above them were guitars hanging. Toward the back of the store was the drum section. A couple demo kits were set up for testing cymbals, heads, or whatever you preferred. Directly in the middle of the store along the wall was a little glass counter with a door that led to the back. He had a great selection of guitars from Dean to Fender to Ibanez. They also had a nice little price tag attached to them. Then the door behind the counter swung open, and out came this old man who was probably in his sixties. He was wearing a white button-up shirt with suspenders holding his blue jeans. I was assuming that this guy was Dick.

"Hello, sir, what can I help you with today?" he asked.

"Oh, I was wondering if you might have seen someone lately with a Fender acoustic guitar? I was robbed last night, and the bastards took my only guitar that meant everything to me."

"I'm so sorry to hear that, son. Do you have a picture of the guitar just in case they do come in?"

"No, sir, I don't."

He replied, "Well, I'll tell you what, my name is Dick Newman, and this is my music shop. Please feel free to look around and play any guitar you want. I know it's not fun having your stuff stolen, but maybe I could help you get a new guitar to replace it."

"I can play any guitar I want?"

"Yes, you sure can, but just be careful."

I walked over to the wall where most of them were hanging. I saw all different makes and models. He had acoustics and electrics, but I was looking for a Gibson Les Paul like what Sebastian was talking about. I didn't see any, so I grabbed this electric Fender Stratocaster. I sat down and plugged it in to this little practice amp that Dick had set up for people trying guitars out. The guitar felt nice. The strings sat closer to the frets, and the neck was so smooth compared to what I've been playing on. After about ten minutes with this thing, I was extremely comfortable. I was tearing it up when Dick approached me.

"Wow, kid, you can really play," he said.

"Thanks, I played for three straight years every day in prison."

I tried to stop myself from saying *prison*, but it was too late. I didn't want anyone to know I went to prison, but I slipped up.

"I'm not going to judge you. I am sixty-two years old, and we all have made bad decisions before, including me. So you must have been doing good in prison if they let you learn guitar."

"Yeah, I just did some dumb shit and had to pay the hard way. I straightened up quickly once I got locked up, plus I met an innocent inmate named John. He helped guide me to the right path, and I made a promise to take this talent as far as I can."

Dick seemed to take interest in wanting to know a little more about myself. So I sat there with him for about two hours and told him most of everything from my childhood to prison to living under a bridge. After our long talk, he said, "Come with me, David, I want to show you something." So I put the guitar back and followed him behind the counter to the door that led to the back. We went through the door that led to his little workshop where he repaired guitars. He asked me to hang here for a second, while he dug through this old closet storage space that was not big enough for the both of us. He then pulled out this old guitar case and sat it on his workbench. Dick brushed the dust off and opened it. In the case sat a beautiful custom Fender Stratocaster electric guitar. It had his last name Newman carved into the headstock. It had beautiful rose thorns laid into the fretwork along with an amazing cherry-rose paint finish on the main body.

Dick said to me, "I built this for my son eight years ago before he passed away. I put David Gilmour pickups in it. If you don't know who that is, he is the lead guitar player for Pink Floyd."

"This is an amazing-looking guitar, and I bet it sounds nasty. If you don't mind, how did you lose your son?"

"He died of a drug overdose. He was only twenty-seven years old. He was my only son, and I was divorced at the time, so he was the only one I was close to. He was a very good guitar player and had a lot going for him and his band."

"I am sorry to hear that."

"Took awhile to heal, but I'm OK now. You remind me a lot of my son. Hey, I want to show you something else. Follow me."

So Dick and I walked back out into the shop and headed out the front door. He put a "return in ten minutes" sign on the door. We walked around to the back of his shop. There was an alley right next to the shop, which was the quickest way considering he had no back door. Once we got around the back of the shop, I followed him down these concrete steps that led to another door. He pulled out his key chain and began fumbling with keys looking for the right one. As soon as I walked in, I saw this very tiny apartment space, not much bigger than the prison cell I stayed in. It had an old pullout couch up against the wall to your right as soon as you walked in the door. The walls were concrete with half the paint chipping off. Across from the couch was a small busted-up wooden television stand with a box television on top. The carpet on the floor was brown with dark stains all over it. I did see a toilet with a small sink attached to the main room.

"My son used to stay here when he was traveling with his band. There was no need for him to get an apartment since he was always gone. So we turned this into a small one-person living space. If you want, you can stay here until you get on your feet."

I said, "Oh, man, you don't have to do that for me, I'm a loser."

"Don't say that about yourself. I am a good judge of character. I see the drive in your heart, and from what you told me and how you were playing, I can tell you want it. Plus, you don't need to be living under a bridge."

"Dick, this means a lot to me, and how can I make it up to you?"

"Just help me clean the shop up a couple days a week, that's all. I will give you two months' rent free. I will give you one key, and you can come and go as you please, just don't leave anything on while you're gone. There is no shower, but if I were you, I would just use soap and a rag for now, and that should get you by."

I was so appreciative for what Dick had done for me. It started with looking for my guitar to getting a roof over my head.

CHAPTER 8

The Unnamed Feeling

Next Thursday, it was time for open jam again at Dino's. I was hoping Sebastian wasn't going to stand me up. I also really needed him to bring his guitar, so I could play. Once I got to Dino's around 9:00 PM, they were just finishing setting up the stage. The drums were up, and the amps were plugged in. I waited to sign up until Sebastian got there. Sure enough, nine thirty rolled around, and here came Sebastian with a guitar case in his hands. He walked in and yelled, "David, my man, you made it!"

"I told you I would be here dude, and I see you held up your end of the bargain."

"I sure did, but where is your acoustic guitar?" Sebastian said.

I paused for a second and then sighed, "Someone stole my guitar last week, and it's gone."

"Oh, man, I am sorry to hear that, people can be real pieces of shit sometimes. Well, I made you a promise, and I will let you rock out on this." Sebastian then opened this case, and it was like opening Pandora's box of love. This guitar was slick-looking.

"This is one of my children, she don't get out much, but don't you just love that desert-burst paint finish?"

I was at a loss for words. This baby had to be well over a couple grand.

He said with a firm tone of voice, "Now, you be careful, you break the guitar, I break your neck. Now let's go sign up."

The same drummer and bassist that came last time were here again. They hosted the open jam, and most of the stuff on stage were theirs. The music flowed, and another great night of music started to unfold. When I got on stage with Sebastian, I plugged the Gibson into a Marshall half stack. After the amp head was warmed up, I turned the volume up. You could just feel the distortion vibrating through my chest. I turned around and looked at Sebastian while nodding my head up and down. He had a smile on his face like he knew what was about to happen. The two of us gave it hell that night, and the drummer and bassist were all about it. I was having so much fun I didn't want to stop or slow down.

Didn't take long before the night had to come to an end, and when I was putting Sebastian's guitar away, he approached me and said, "Hey, what are you doing after here?"

"Nothing, really, just going back to my place for now I guess."

"How would you like to come over to my place and jam some more?" he asked.

"Sure thing, dude, it beats going home and doing nothing."

He threw his hands up, "Well, what the hell are we waiting for? Grab your shit, and let's go."

We jumped in his little beat-up Toyota car and went back to his place. I arrived at this tiny, little house, which I thought was a shack because it was so small. As I walked in the front door, his whole house was nothing but rock 'n' roll. He had a small drum kit in the corner along with small amps scattered everywhere. There was a PA system all hooked up with floor monitors. Rock 'n' roll and naked-girl posters all over the walls. He had a small dirty couch with potato-chip crumbs all over it and a box TV with rabbit ears. The kitchen was attached to the main room on the back left side of the room. In the middle was a hallway that led to the bathroom and his room.

Sebastian turned his head, "Well, what do you think?"

"I like it a lot, dude, I really do."

"I call it rock 'n' roll paradise," Sebastian said.

Sebastian literally eats, shits, and breathes rock 'n' roll music. "Grab a seat on the couch, and let me get you a beer," he insisted.

The couch was more filthy than mine, but I wasn't expecting his place to look like a Hollywood dream house either. So I took a seat on the couch while he got me a Budweiser.

"So David you got any original material?" he asked.

"Yeah, I got some stuff but not a lot."

"Well, let me jump on the microphone here, and see what we can work out."

I hooked up to one of his amps and began to play. I started playing some riffs that I wrote while he stood there and listened. Sebastian then got behind the microphone and began humming melodies. It didn't take long before words started following. He was a great singer, and his melodies were amazing. Just twenty minutes in, and we damn near had a full song written. After that, he looked at me and said, "David, have you ever played in a band before? You have a unique style and it sounds awesome."

"No, but I really want to. I don't think I am that good yet to be in a band."

He was quick to fire back, "Oh, shut the hell up, are you kidding me? You are a very talented man. How would you like to start a band with me?"

"If you're serious, dude, I really want to. I don't know much, but I am a quick learner. How are we going to get a drummer and a bassist?"

Sebastian replied as he laughed, "I haven't thought that far ahead yet. However, I used to play with this drummer and bassist back in the day. Let me call them up tomorrow, and I'm sure they will be very interested especially when they hear you play. I do want to get to know you a little more. I have never seen you around town before, so where did you come from, and how did you get so good because that doesn't come overnight?"

I knew that question was going to come eventually, but I wasn't sure if I should lie to him as it could end up bad in the end, so I had to be real with him, "If I tell you, you promise not to freak out and throw me out?"

"Oh, shit, you're a wanted murderer." Sebastian started chuckling and followed up with, "I am kidding, but there is a lot that I've been through too, so I'm sure it's not that bad. I have all night plus more beer, so please fill me in. Plus, if we're going to be in a serious band, I would like to know, and I promise your word is safe with me."

I went on, "Oh, where do I start? Um, I was raised in an orphan home just outside of Cleveland. I became a troublemaker at a young age, and through my teens, I got involved with drug hustling. I wasn't addicted to the drugs myself, but I found a way to make good money out of it. Sleeping with girls became a very simple process especially when they wanted to get really high. It started to consume my life, and before I knew it, I got busted selling to an undercover cop and got locked away at Oaksville Penitentiary."

Sebastian jumped in and said, "Oh, damn, dude, you went there? I heard that was home to some nasty boys."

"Yeah, the judge thought that would scare the hell out of me and straighten me up. I saw things in prison that I thought I would never see. I met an innocent man who was my cellmate. That place was hell on earth, and I barely survived. I was sentenced for five years. After my first year there, I managed to get on the good list, and so I was rewarded. That's how I learned to play music. It eventually got to the point where I was so respected for the music that they released me early. That guitar, Sebastian, that you saw me play last week was given to me by the prison."

"Sorry to interrupt, but who the hell stole it? 'Cause that pisses me off," Sebastian said.

I went on again, "Some bums passing through. I drifted here after prison and was sleeping under that bridge where the railroad tracks are just on the other side of town. They got me when I was sleeping. Then, I met Dick who has the music store, and I told him my situation like I'm telling you, and he was nice enough to give me a small place to crash until I got on my feet. So, Sebastian, that's pretty much all of it in a nutshell, and now I'm here."

He said, "Holy shit, that is some crazy shit. I am glad to hear that Dick helped you out. He is just a cool guy, and did he tell you about his son?"

"Yes, he did, and that's sad."

Then, Sebastian paused for a second and took a big swig of beer and said, "Well, I know things happen for a reason, and I am glad you are here. You're more than welcome to use my equipment when you are here. I know you don't have much, but good things are coming your way, and I can feel it.

"I guess it's my turn to tell you a little bit about myself. I had many ups and downs in my household when I was young. My dad was a hardworking man who owned a very small mechanic shop at the time. We didn't have a whole lot of money, but that didn't bother me because my dad was my best friend until his freak accident happened."

"Oh, shit, what happened?" I blurted.

"He was working on a 1972 Buick four-door sedan. He was leaning over the engine compartment and revving its engine when it backfired, and one of five aluminum blades from its fan broke free and struck him in the side of his head. He barely survived, but his head injury was so severe that he was never the same again. It definitely messed his brain up. My mother worked at a small diner just around the corner from here. She had to bust her ass just to make ends meet. While this was going on, my dad became a raging alcoholic and started beating my mom. She would just sit there and take it almost every other night. Afterward, she would just break down in tears. I could hear the cries coming from the bedroom. I didn't know what to do, so I sat there and watched him do that for a couple years. Wasn't long after that I started singing. Singing and lyric writing was my way of coping with the anger toward my dad. She finally got smart and filed for divorce after the night I punched him in the jaw. I loved my dad, but he was never the same since the accident. I went and lived with my mom until I was eighteen, and then I moved out. This is my grandma's old place I turned into my rock 'n' roll palace. Rock 'n' roll is my life now, and I will pursue it till the day I die. I currently work for a small landscaping company. I cut grass, weed whack, and lay mulch in the early season. Not what I want to spend the rest of my life doing, but it pays my bills for now. So, David, that is my story in a nutshell."

I looked at him and said, "I guess we both have crazy backgrounds, and I am sorry all that happened to you, but I agree that things do happen for a reason. I can't wait to write some killer tunes and help you chase this dream."

"Thank you, I know we will kick some major ass together."

The night was getting late, and I had one hell of a buzz. I said, "Hey, man, I am starting to get tired, would you mind taking me back to my place?"

"Dude, if you want, you can crash here, and drink some more beer if you want."

I said, "Nah, I have had way too many for the night, plus it's your beer. So if it's cool, I will crash right here on the couch. Oh, and by the way, you might find a few sticky spots on your couch or carpet."

I had to throw some humor in there, and he just laughed and said, "OK, but I will kick your ass from here all the way back to your place. Anyhow, I am heading to bed too. Good night, David, and I will see you in the morning."

"Good night, Sebastian," I replied.

He then went down the hallway to his room. When morning came around, I overheard Sebastian talking on the phone in the kitchen. It sounded like he had called one of the guys we talked about last night. I lay there and listened, "Hey, Marc, you still drumming for that band called Sister Mister?" Then there were pauses because I couldn't hear what the other guy was saying. "Oh, you're not, well, that's cool, but I got this guy I met named David, and he is a damn good guitar player. He is pretty serious about his music, so what do you say you come over sometime and jam with us for the hell of it." Another pause, "Oh, hell, yeah, dude, you won't be disappointed, I promise. OK, Monday evening sounds good, I will see you then and take care." He hung up the phone and came over where I was lying down.

"Rise and shine, pumpkin tits, I got this drummer named Marc coming over to jam with us on Monday."

"Pumpkin tits?" as I looked at him all confused.

"As you get to know me a little more, you will notice I say the most random things when I get excited. Most men get a boner, I say random dumb shit that sounds funny."

All I could say back to that was, "I'm not going to argue, whatever floats your boat. So I will be here whatever time you need me."

CHAPTER 9

All Within My Hands

When Monday rolled around, I had Sebastian pick me up in front of the music store. On the way there, we stopped for some McDonald's. He bought me a Big Mac with a Coke. That tasted amazing compared to the nasty prison food I had been sucking down. Once we arrived at his place, I helped him straighten a few things up and got everything ready. I was plugging in his Gibson when I heard someone knocking on the front door. Sebastian went over and answered it. A guy standing 5'11" with a baby face and long brown hair was standing at the door. He had tight blue jeans while wearing a Kiss T-shirt.

Sebastian said, "What's up, Marc? So glad you could make it. Come on in, did you bring your drum kit, or do you want to use mine?"

Marc replied as he stepped in, "Well, of course, I brought my kit. I don't like the beginner kit you have. Hey, is this the guitar player you were talking about? Hello, man, my name is Marc Allenhart."

We both reached out and shook hands as I introduced myself as well. "Hey, Marc, nice to meet you, my name is David."

Sebastian and Marc then went to his car to get his drum kit. This drum kit was sweet; it had a badass custom flame job on the kick drum along with shiny new cymbals. It took Marc a few minutes to get set up, and after that, we jumped right into jamming. We were about twenty minutes in when I thought I heard someone else screaming at the door. I stopped and asked both of them if they were hearing someone, and before we knew it, the front door comes flying wide open. A man holding a guitar case with black pants with chains and a vest that said "Who's your daddy?" on the back started yelling. "Damn, Sebastian, I have been standing out front for so long the hair on my balls is turning gray!"

The room was completely quiet after that. Then, Sebastian yelled, "If it ain't Anthony Wildman Martini, my cousin from another dozen. I was wondering when the hell you were going to show up!"

"Sorry, I was running late, my girl wanted to take a ride on my disco stick, and I couldn't refuse. I heard you got a killer new guitar player, Sebastian, is this him?"

I reached out again and introduced myself to Anthony. Anthony then said, "I am a bass player, and my job is to provide that bottom end that vibrates the hell out of the walls. Nothing is better than that rumble in the jungle, especially for the ladies." My first impression of Anthony was that he seemed very open. He had some humor in him, and I laughed when he said that.

After all was said and done and the introducing of each other was over, we had a band and began to see how well we could work together. We started off with a few covers to warm up. There was a lot of pressure on me because I was the only guitar player. So I bit my lip and gave it everything I had. As I looked around the room, I could see some smiles on their faces. I had chills running up and down my neck. After about four songs, Marc and Anthony were like, "Damn, Sebastian, where did you find this guy?"

"I like him, he has some talent. He also has some sex appeal too. Let me tell you that will come in handy down the road," Anthony said.

"Guys, that's why I called you because I knew you would be impressed."

"I think we are on to something here," Marc commented.

"I got butterflies, boys, I really do. Let's try and write a couple originals. David, go ahead and play those riffs we worked on the other day," Sebastian mentioned.

So I began to play those couple riffs back to back that I had, and then Marc came in with a simple beat along with Anthony's bass. Sebastian then busted out his lyrics and began singing to it. So far, we were off to a great start. I was providing some backup vocals along with Anthony. I was starting to really get the hang of things. After about three hours of nonstop rock 'n' roll, we had almost three originals complete. The juices were flowing, and our chemistry was getting tight. So we all sat down together and discussed everything from music to our future goals.

Sebastian started out, "I would like to say that was an awesome jam session today. I am very serious about this and would like to take this to the next level. I want to know what you guys are thinking."

Marc was sitting behind his drum set and said, "I am only twenty-three years old, and music has been a huge part of my life. Things didn't work out for my last band Sister Mister, so I am in."

We all looked over at Anthony as he said, "You know, guys, I'm not sure, I might lead you on for nine months and drop out. I really like working these temp jobs, plus I might end up marrying a chubby bitch because I heard they cook good food."

We all stared at him as if he was being serious, then he yelled, "I am kidding, dudes, let's fucking rock!"

Then at that very moment, our band Amerex was founded. A heavy distortion sound with a raspy outlaw singer. The four of us started practicing four to five hours every other night. During these times, I got to know Marc and Anthony on a more personal level. Marc was raised by strict parents, and they hated rock 'n' roll. His mom thought rock 'n' roll was the devil's music. He started playing drums when he was eight years old. He would drum on cardboard boxes until he saved up enough money to get his first real kit. The resentment from his parents pushed him into doing it more. Once he got really good, his parents started to ease up after he blew the doors off at his high school talent show. He works at a local restaurant as a waiter.

Anthony was the definition of a troublemaker. If you were to look up *troublemaker* in the dictionary, there would be a picture of Anthony. His mother is only sixteen years older than him because his father is in prison for sleeping with a minor. So he lacks a little discipline, but he is very dedicated to his bass playing. He constantly jumps from one job to the next. He tends to get fired from every job, but we know where his heart is. His main influences were Van Halen, Black Sabbath, and Led Zeppelin.

Sebastian's biggest inspirations were Metallica, Ozzy, and Guns N' Roses.

Marc loved Kiss, Rush, and Dream Theater.

We were not just a band; we were becoming a family with a dream.

Things started looking up for me. I helped Dick keep his store maintained, and he would throw me a little cash under the table here and there. I cleaned up my living space and painted the walls for him to show my appreciation. I was in the store one day cleaning and was so excited about it I had to mentioned to him that I joined a band, and he said, "Oh, that's awesome, David, I knew it wouldn't be long before someone found you. Just know that it's a tough business, but if you keep a level head, you will do just fine."

"Thanks, Dick, for helping me get on my feet. You're a good man no matter what anyone says," I said.

About an hour later I was at the back of the store when I heard the doorbell ring, and this man came in carrying an acoustic guitar. I did a double take and then realized that it was my guitar. The son of a bitch came in to sell my guitar to Dick. The man said, "Hi, sir, would you be interested in buying a guitar?"

I damn near bit my lip off in anger. I slowly walked up behind the man and tried to signal Dick that that was my guitar.

Dick said to him, "Oh, well, let me take a look at it, and I will think about it."

As Dick was examining the guitar, he looked over and saw me signaling him. He winked at me letting me know he got the message.

"You sure this is your guitar?"

"Yeah, old man, this is my guitar."

"Why are you wanting to sell it?" Dick asked.

"Because I need money, so how much will you take for it?" he demanded.

I clinched my fists and was about to act, but then Dick said, "OK, here is my deal, buddy. You see that man behind you?" pointing in my direction.

The man turned his head and glanced at me and then turned back to Dick. "Yeah, what about that guy?"

"This guitar matches the description of a guitar that was stolen, and it belongs to that man. So you have two options. One, I will give you ten bucks, and I will keep the guitar, and you will leave my store and never return. Two, I will have him kick your ass if you refuse my first offer and hold you down until the cops get here. So what's it going to be, partner?"

The man seemed really scared as he took the ten bucks and ran out the door. I looked at Dick and said, "I really wanted to kick his ass."

"I know you did, but look at the good side of it. We got your guitar back. Trust me you won't see that guy anytime soon."

I started to calm down and was grateful for that idiot bringing it in. Dick took the guitar for a couple days to do some minor repairs. It needed new strings, and the neck had to be reset. That guitar had a lot of sentimental value to me, and I couldn't be more happy that I finally got it back.

CHAPTER 10

Hit the Lights

A couple of weeks went by, and I met up with the guys to discuss getting our first real gig. We met back at Sebastian's place to toss around ideas. I said, "What do you guys think about going down to Dino's and getting a gig there?"

Marc replied, "Dino's would be an awesome spot, but Danny, the general manager, is an asshole when it comes to booking bands in there. If you don't bring a crowd, you can kiss that gig goodbye."

Sebastian said, "I know I have never met him, but I heard the same thing from a buddy of mine. David and I rocked that place when they had open jam, but there were only about twenty-five people in there at the most, and that's not a big-enough crowd to talk Danny into it."

Anthony butted in, "What the hell, is it going to hurt if we went down there and asked his mean ass? The worst thing he can say is no."

The four of us packed into Marc's Chevy Astro van and traveled down to Dino's Bar 'n' Grill to talk to Danny. Once we arrived, we asked the bartender if we could speak to Danny. She told us to wait a second as she went into the back to get him. Danny came out from the back. He was this skinny, little nerdy guy wearing a polo shirt and black slacks. He said, "Can I help you, gentlemen?"

Here we were, the four of us dressed like dirty rockers. Sebastian said, "Our band Amerex would like to play a show here. Me and this guy here have played in here during your open jam."

Danny replied, "Yeah, I've heard you sing before. You're good, but not that good. Look, guys, I get amateur bands in here all the time, bugging me to headline their own show or open up for a big act. I am going to be honest with you, this is a business, and I have to make money, and you don't even have a CD or a band resume put together so you are wasting your time. Now I have to get back to doing what I was doing. Have a nice day, boys."

Sebastian fired right back with anger, "OK, asshole, I will make you a deal right now! If we bring one hundred people through that door, you can keep all the alcohol and door sales. We just want to play a damn show!"

Danny stepped back like he was scared we were going to jump the bar and kick his ass. He paused for a second and said, "OK, you guys seem hungry, I will take that bet, but if you don't bring at least one hundred people through that door, you can kiss your asses good-bye on ever playing a show here. I am trying to run a business here."

Sebastian came back with, "What if we do bring the people, what will you do in return?"

"I will let you open for a national act and pay you one hundred dollars. Your show will be on the last Friday of this month. That will give you about three weeks, so it looks like you boys have work to do."

Sebastian reached his hand out and shook hands with Danny.

As we headed back out the front door, Anthony yelled, "What a little queer, he acts like he is a badass in there, but I bet his wife beats him when he gets home!"

The rest of us just burst out laughing. Sebastian said, "How about we go get something to eat and discuss how the hell we are going to get one hundred people through that door?"

The four of us jumped back into Marc's van and headed to that diner I ate when I first arrived here. We walked in, and the hostess sat all of us in a booth near the window. That waitress, Erica, was our server. She said, "Hello, boys, my name is Erica, and what could I start you off to drink?"

Anthony and Marc both ordered coffee with cream. Sebastian ordered a sweet tea with no lemon. I ordered a Coke, and she looked right at me and said, "Hey, good to see you again, how was the open jam that night?"

"It was fun, I met this guy sitting next to me, and now I am in a band with these guys."

"Oh, that's awesome. I will have to come check you guys out sometime soon. Let me go get your drinks real fast, and I will be back to take your order."

She walked away for a second, and Anthony said to me, "Dude, that girl is pretty sexy, and I think she likes you, David."

"No, she doesn't."

"Did you not pay attention to the way she was looking at you?" he said.

Sebastian leaned over, "Yeah, I did see that, and we should definitely get her to come to the show. You never know, David, you might get a piece of ass once she hears you play."

I was getting a little embarrassed. I said to the guys, "Oh, knock it off, she don't want to date some loser guitar player like me."

"I bet ten dollars that she will come to the show if you ask her," Sebastian said.

"I will bet ten dollars too," Marc added.

"OK, just let the bet go, guys. I will ask her before we leave, I promise."

"Yeah, that's my boy!" Sebastian shouted.

Then out of nowhere, Anthony said, "I got it, guys. I know how we can get people through the door."

"Free beer," he announced.

"Are you retarded, how is that possible?" Sebastian asked.

"We make up a bunch of flyers for the show. At the bottom of the flyer, we put in very small letters featuring our new single 'Free Beer.' The 'Free Beer' will be in large letters, and that's all that will stand out on the flyer. So everyone who reads the flyer will think they are getting free beer at the show."

"I can see that causing some major problems," I said.

"I like it, bad publicity is good publicity," Marc announced.

Sebastian said, "Let's do it, if we are going to be a rock band, then it's time we start acting like one. In the words of Lou Reed, let's take a walk on the wild side."

So we had a game plan, and we were going to stick to it. When all was said and done and we were done eating, our waitress came to give us our check for the food. I manned up in front of the guys and asked her out.

"Erica, would you like to come to our show, and maybe have dinner with me before?" I mumbled.

The guys all had this goofy look on their faces as she replied, "Are you asking me out on a date?"

"Um, yes, I am."

She didn't even hesitate, "I would like that. Here is my number, so you can call me whenever you want." She pulled out a pen, wrote her number on a tissue, and then handed it to me. She smiled and walked away. The guys were patting me on the back and telling me that I was going to get some booty soon. There's one thing these guys love, and that's women.

Anthony leaned over and said, "Hey, you know, if you hook up with that and would like to swing, my girlfriend is all into that."

"Um, yeah, buddy, let me think about that."

"Hey, I'm just saying only if you're into that," he said.

We paid the check and went back to Sebastian's place. We started making these handmade flyers that said "Amerex Live at Dino's." The "free beer" stuck out like a sore thumb, but that was our plan. At the end of the day, I went back to my place and stared at the phone number on the tissue. I didn't have a phone down here. The only access I had to a phone was either a pay phone or the phone in Dick's store. I never really liked any girl until I met her. Something inside me felt like she might be the one for me.

CHAPTER 11

Prince Charming

The next morning, I waited until Dick opened the store so I could use his phone. I bolted through the front door, and he said, "Wow, look like you're in a hurry."

I replied as I was breathing heavily, "Yeah, Dick, I have to use your phone." I ran behind his shop and started dialing her digits. Three rings and I heard a voice say, "Hello."

"Hi, is this Erica?"

"Yes, it is. Who is this?"

"This is David from the diner the other day. I was with my band, and you gave me your number."

"Oh, hi, darling, how are you?"

"I'm doing good, how about yourself?"

"Oh, things are good now that you called."

She giggled after she said that. Then I said, "So do you still want to go out on a date with me?"

"Oh, course I do, darling."

I cupped the phone and then pulled it away from my ear and yelled yes really loud through the back of the store. I then presumed, "OK, great, when would be the best time for you?"

"How about this Friday around 8:00 PM?"

"Friday at eight sounds great. What is your address?"

She answered, "My address is 201 South Baker Ave, Apartment B." I struggled to find a pen so I could write it down. Once I found one, I said, "Awesome, I can't wait to see you. Hey, I got to get back to taking care of the store, but I will see you soon."

"OK, darling, same to you, and I will see you Friday, goodbye."

I said goodbye and hung up the phone. I was walking on cloud nine. I went back out to the front of the store while Dick was hanging up a couple guitars. He looked over at me and said, "I think I know what that's all about. Did you meet a girl?"

"Yes, sir, I did! She is a pretty waitress named Erica who works at that diner not far from here."

Dick was excited for me as he said, "That is great to hear, David, and correct me if I am wrong, but did I overhear you say you were going to meet her at her place?"

"Yeah, I was going to walk over to her place considering I don't have a car."

"I tell you what, if you can cover the shop for the next couple of days, I have to go out of town for some business stuff. I will lend you my truck on Friday and throw you a few extra bucks so you can take her somewhere decent. You don't want to leave a bad impression on your first date with this pretty girl."

"Come on, Dick, you don't have to do that for me. You have done enough for me already."

"You have been helping me out for a while now, and it would be my pleasure to give you another hand. Do you have a driver's license?"

"Yes, I got my license when I was sixteen."

"OK then, you need to cover the shop tomorrow and Thursday from ten to six PM." I told him I would be here right at 10:00 AM.

Over the next couple days, I cleaned the store so well that there was not one speck of dust. I went as far as buffing the floors and washing the front windows. I had all the guitars off the wall and cleaned along with the amplifiers. When it was time to close, I made sure all the doors were locked, and then I would head off to practice. Dick arrived Friday afternoon and was very impressed with the way the store looked. He ended up giving me fifty bucks, and that was more than I needed. The truck he was lending me was a Chevy S-10 extended cab. The truck was red with a killer sound system. To me this was styling, but to him it was a piece of shit. I don't think he was a Chevy fan. I used his computer to look up the address and found out how to get there on MapQuest. I dressed as nice as I could and shaved my face. I kept my long hair because it matches the image of the band. It was 8:00 PM, and I pulled up to this house on Baker Avenue. It was a double-story house that was split into two apartments. I got out of the car and walked up to the porch. There was a divider in the middle of the porch that divided each side. The left side said apartment A on the door, and the right side said apartment B. I knocked on apartment B. I heard a woman yell, "Just a second, be right there!"

I waited for a few seconds. Then the door opened, and there stood Erica. She had her hair down and was wearing a Pink Floyd shirt. Her jeans were supertight as I stood there in shock. She was so beautiful I was speechless. I mumbled, "Wow, you look great, Erica."

"Thanks, hun, you look cute in your rocker clothes. So is that your truck?"

"Yes, that is mine, so you ready to go?"

"Of course, let me grab my stuff, and I will meet you at the truck."

I went back and waited by the truck as she got her stuff. She came out, and off we went. As we were driving, she said, "So where are you taking me?"

"If I told you, it would ruin the surprise," I said.

I pulled up to a place called Cherry Street Pub. Dick recommended that I take her there. Erica said to me, "Oh, you're taking me here? I've heard good things about this place."

As soon as we walked in, a hostess said, "How many?"

"Two and can we have a booth if that's OK?" I requested.

"Sure, right this way."

The place looked very nice. It had nice polished hardwood floors with a granite top bar that was connected to the dining room. They also had picture frames of famous movies hanging on the walls. The place was very nice, and that made me nervous about the food prices because I didn't have that much. Once we got seated, she handed us our menus and said a waitress would be right with us. The menu prices weren't too bad at all, so I eased up.

Erica looked at the menu and said, "Wow, the food looks delicious, thank you for taking me here."

"You're welcome, get whatever you want."

A waitress then came over and took our order. We both ordered a tall ice-cold Bud Light.

"I think I am going to get the Cherry Pub burger," Erica commented.

"Yeah, that looks really good, so I think I am going to get the same thing."

The waitress took our order and brought us our Bud Lights. This was the time to get to know Erica, and our entire dinner conversation went like this. "So what made you want to ask me out? And be honest."

She smiled at me as I replied, "Well, I thought you seemed very nice, and I think you are the most attractive woman I have ever seen. Plus the guys kept calling me a pussy, and that finally made me do it."

"Aww, thank you, and some of the guys are cute, but you are the cutest by far. So tell me a little about yourself and how long have you been in a band?"

I was not going to tell her about prison, so I made up a lie. "Oh, where do I start? I never met my real parents. They were deceased, and I spent my youth living with my foster parents. I never listened to them, and all I would do is run around with my friends and do dumb shit. You know kids will be kids. Once I got into my teens, I began to experiment with drugs and started to head down the wrong path. When I was eighteen, I had to move out and get away from all the trouble. I spent the next four years bouncing around. The real world was tough, and I needed another fresh new start, so I moved here. That was the first day I met you at your work, and you told me to get to Dino's. After I went there, I met Sebastian, and we just hit it off. Then he introduced me to the other two, and now we are a band. It's crazy how it all worked out, and now we have that show at Dino's coming up soon. I love music, and this is my first real band and first real show as the lead guitar player."

Erica said, "Wow, that's really exciting, and I am sorry about your parents."

"That's OK, I never met them, so it is what it is. So, Erica, please tell me a little bit about yourself and how a pretty girl like you doesn't have a boyfriend?"

She went on to explain, "I always seem to pick the assholes. My ex-boyfriend was a complete tool bag, and I had to get out of the relationship. I lived here my whole life and had a good life growing up with my family and sister. I just work at the diner to help pay for my schooling."

I jumped in and said, "Oh, cool, what is your major?"

"I am studying to be a veterinarian. I am a big animal lover, and I want to help as much as I can. I want to open my own clinic once school is over."

"That's awesome, I really hope you pull it off. Can I ask you another question?"

"Yes, of course."

"What made you want to go on this date with a long-haired rocker? And be honest."

She blushed and answered, "Oh, you asked me too fast, I normally don't date rockers because they sleep with every girl who takes off their pants. However, you seem different. I can't seem to put my finger on it yet."

"Well, I will tell you that I am not like the average everyday rocker," I replied.

We both laughed, and so far, we had our food scarfed down and were three or four beers in. Erica said, "Oh, I am getting quite a little buzz, how about you?"

I replied, "Yeah, I got a good buzz going. What would you like to do after we leave here?"

She leaned over the table and whispered, "How about we go back to my place and maybe watch a movie?"

I was certain that was code for something else. I said, "Yeah, sure, that sounds great."

I paid for the bill, and we went back to her place. The whole time on the way back, she kept rubbing my right thigh and giving me this sexy look. My pants were getting extremely uncomfortable. I thought my zipper was going to burst. Once we got back, I had trouble getting out of the truck and walking through the front door. We went straight upstairs to her room. I had mentioned to her what movie she wanted to watch, and the only response I got was her closing the bedroom door and taking her shirt off. She then pushed me on to her bed and jumped on top of me. Her hair was covering my face as we started making out. I tried to speak to her, but she put her finger on my lips and whispered in my ear, "We didn't come here to watch a movie."

Erica then reached into my jeans and grabbed my penis. That was a clear signal to me what she was after. I took off my shirt as she was unbuttoning my pants. I was lying on my back and staring at the ceiling. I could feel her pulling my pants off. My cock was so hard as she started going down on me. I moaned and I moaned as she continued for the next five minutes. She was doing things with her tongue that I never thought was possible. After that, she got off the edge of the bed and stood up to take her pants off. She was standing there topless with this sexy pink thong on. She then slowly started to take her thong off. I was stroking myself as she was doing this. I was about to go exploring Pandora's box of love. She asked, "Do you have any condoms?"

I was hesitant to reply because I never carried condoms on me. Took me a second, but I replied, "No, sorry, I don't." She paused like I did and thought it through. She said, "Oh, well, fuck it, just don't cum in me, or I will beat your ass."

"I won't, I promise," I said.

She then got in bed with me, and we went at it. I hadn't been with a woman in over four years, so I had to stop every couple of minutes because I was going to blow. Ten minutes into, she said to me, "David, I want you to put your hands around my neck and choke me."

I was on top of her in a mercenary position. So I put both hands around her neck and started choking her. She would moan to me, "Harder, baby, choke me harder, baby!" It was getting extremely intense, and when I closed my eyes, images started flashing through my head. I saw the black men holding me down in the shower. I shook my head and opened my eyes. Erica was still telling me to give it to her harder.

I tried closing my eyes again, and then I saw the images flashing again and heard the men laughing as I was crying. I bit down on my lip, and then I squeezed as hard as I could. I could hear them laughing in my head, and so I squeezed and I squeezed until I felt a hand smacking the edge of the bed. I opened my eyes, and her face was getting blue. I quickly snapped out of it, and let go of her. She gasped heavily for air as she rolled out from underneath of me. I said in a panic as she was coughing heavily, "Oh my gosh, I am so sorry, Erica, I didn't know how hard you wanted it!"

She replied, "Jesus, dude, you could have made me pass out, what the fuck is your problem? I didn't mean that hard. You looked like you were having a seizure, are you OK?"

I said, "I'm sorry, I don't know what got into me. You kept saying harder and harder, and so I did what you said." I didn't mention a word about the images I was seeing in my head. It probably would have freaked her out. I was suffering from posttraumatic stress syndrome, and I wasn't going to say anything. After the situation calmed down, she said to me, "Oh, well, I guess it's kinda my fault too for telling you. How about you come over and finish on me, and we call it a night."

I replied in a sexy voice, "OK, babe, sounds good." We got into a very sexy position, and then I ejaculated, and that was it for me. I rolled over all sweaty and breathing heavily. She looked over at me and said, "Not bad, not bad at all, David, you left quite a mess."

"Thanks, that was amazing for me," I responded.

Erica reached over and pulled out a cigarette from her purse and started smoking. I sat up and started to get dressed at the edge of the bed when she said to me, "Hey, sorry, but you will have to go soon, my parents will be home."

My eyes got bigger than the moon as I freaked out thinking she was underage. I turned around on the bed and said in a nervous voice, "Did you say your parents were coming home?"

"Yes, I am only nineteen and still live with my parents."

I dodged a major prison sentence thinking she was going to say she was underage. I said, "OK, I better get going, can I call you tomorrow?"

She winked at me. "Maybe."

I said goodbye and hurried my ass out the door and got in the truck. Once I was in the truck, I looked in the rearview mirror and said to myself, "Yeah, who's the man? I am."

CHAPTER 12

Free Speech for the Dumb

The big show was coming up, and we had to start practicing. Right before practice, Sebastian said, "So, David, how was your date with Erica?"

"Yeah, you get any ass out of it?" Anthony commented.

"Yes, I did, I took her to dinner, and afterward, she said she wanted to go back to her place to watch a movie. We ended up going straight to the bedroom and got it on. I have been trying to call her, but she hasn't been returning my calls. I think she is ignoring me."

Marc burst into laughter and said, "I can't hold it in, guys, I just can't."

Then Sebastian and Anthony started laughing out loud as well. I was confused and said, "What in the hell is so funny? Is there something I need to know about this girl?"

Anthony was struggling to get out what he wanted to say because of the nonstop laughter. "Hell, yeah, there is something you need to know. She's the town whore, dude. She don't care about you, and we all knew that," Anthony said.

I stood there in shock for a second and said, "Oh, shut the hell up, guys, tell me you're joking, right?"

They continued laughing and shaking their heads no. I raised my voice, "So you're telling me that she does this to guys all the time? So why in the hell did you tell me to ask her out?"

Sebastian said, "You looked like you needed to get your rocks off, dude. When you were in the bathroom at the diner, me and Anthony discussed it, and Marc went along with it."

When I looked over at Marc, he just shrugged his shoulders and agreed. Anthony said, "Did she make up some story about her wanting to be a doctor or veterinarian?"

"How do you know all this?" I asked.

Anthony replied as he was laughing, "Because everyone in this room has slept with her."

I had this disgusting look on my face and said, "Oh my god, I didn't even use a condom. I probably have a disease by now."

Sebastian jumped in and said, "You're good, man, trust me you're good."

"How am I supposed to believe that?"

"Because we are all clean," Marc blurted.

The three of them burst out laughing again. I hung my head for a second, and then I began to laugh along with them. I met my first groupie, and we aren't even famous yet.

After everything got settled down and the jokes were done, it was time for practice. We had a great set list for the show. It was full of mostly covers and originals. The bands that we were going to cover were Guns N' Roses, Motley Crue, Skid Row, and Metallica. Over the whole course of practicing, I developed a unique skill. I could listen to a song a few times and pick out the notes they were playing. The originals were sounding great. We had songs called "Light It Up," "All I Want," and "Shameless." We never really discussed our outfits for the show, and plus we still had to go post all the flyers around town. Sebastian was not a big fan of skinny, tight leather clothing. Marc loved to wear bandanas and eyeliner. Anthony was the only one in the group that had a Mohawk and liked to wear chains all over his torn-up black jeans. I told the guys, "Hey, I don't have much clothes, especially for the stage."

Sebastian said, "That's OK, brother, I got you. I have a good selection of rocker clothes you can pick from. Marc and Anthony, you guys know what to wear, just promise me you won't look gay."

I said, "OK, that's cool, now we have to get off our asses and hang these flyers."

So all four of us grabbed the homemade stack of flyers and got into Marc's van. Our mission was to spread out and hit every light pole and business window within a five-mile radius. With less than two weeks to go, the entire town was going to know about the show. The free-beer scam was an excellent idea by Anthony, but we had to write a song called "Free Beer." It was the stupidest, shortest, and dumbest song ever written, but it was catchy. We were ready and full of rock energy. The guys wanted to take the week off before and not practice because they always thought that practicing right up to the day of the show was bad luck.

During the week off, I continued to do what I do and help Dick keep the store cleaned up. Then he brought up the conversation about how my date went. "So, David, how did things go with you and that Erica girl? And thanks for not wrecking my truck."

"Oh, you're welcome, and to make a long story short, Dick, she was a raging whore who liked the penis, and once she got what she wanted, she disappeared."

He started to laugh and followed up with, "Buddy, let me tell you, I used to be a chick magnet back in the day. I couldn't keep them away so consider yourself lucky. You really have to be careful with women especially because you're in a serious band."

"What do you mean by that?" I asked.

He said, "There are three major things that will destroy a rock band quicker than you can imagine. Number one is women. They will hate the fact that you are in a band, but will not tell you, and they can get very insecure. If there is a hot girl staring you down from the front row as if she wants to fuck and you make eye contact. Boy, oh boy, if your girlfriend sees that, you will never hear the end. Especially if she thinks that girl is prettier than her. Oh, and I forgot, sometimes they will say they love you and only you and want to be with you until the day you die. Then, before you know it, she is banging your drummer or singer. They can cause so much drama between you and the band that it will make your head explode. Number two is drugs and alcohol. This is pretty self-explanatory. Addictions can be a highway to hell, and trust me I know because of my son. Number three is egos. The first person who normally gets the ego is the lead singer. Sometimes it's the guitar player too. Whoever it may be, there is nothing more annoying than someone who thinks they are better than everyone. They become difficult to work with, and afterward, you tend to part ways because you can't deal with the asshole. I have been around music and bands my entire life, and I have seen it and done it all."

"I am assuming you have done your fair share of drugs too?"

"Oh, no, I stayed away from that shit," he replied.

I was just joking a little with him about the drugs, but I forgot about his son. My relationship with Dick was becoming very strong, and he really enjoyed having me around.

CHAPTER 13

St Anger

Showtime, the day was finally here for the four of us. I was up all night due to all the dreams I was having about the show. Load-in time was around 5:00 PM, so we all met at Sebastian's house around two. Marc tore down his drum kit and loaded it up in the back of his trailer that was attached to the van. I didn't know he had a trailer until he showed up that day. These guys have been around the block a few times so they come prepared. I was going to be using Sebastian's guitar and amp for the show. Anthony and I helped each other load the equipment into the trailer. Sebastian had it easy. All he needed was a microphone stand and a mic. We all got dressed up, and off we went. As we pulled up to the back of the bar, I was already starting to get nervous. They had a load-in ramp that was connected to the backstage door, which makes it very easy for bands to get in and out. Sebastian went and met with the manager to get all the details for tonight. The rest of us dropped the trailer door and started loading in the back.

With only a few hours till showtime, everything was going smooth. The sound guy's name was Pat, and he was a laidback pot-smoking hippie. He said through the talk-back microphone as we were on stage, "OK, drummer, I need your kick drum."

So Marc started to stomp his kick drum. Then, he said, "OK, now give me your snare."

Pow, pow, pow went the snare drum. This was my first real sound check, and I was totally fascinated. Once the drum toms were done, it was Anthony's turn then mine. Pat said to Anthony, "OK, give me some bass." When he did that, I could feel the bass rumbling through the stage. Then he said, "All right, give me some of that sweet Les Paul."

I turned up the volume knob on the guitar, and he made it sound so good. I looked over at the guys, and they knew it sounded good. After we were done, it was Sebastian's turn for a vocal check. He yelled into the microphone, "Check one, check two, check one, check two!"

Pat told us we were all good, and as we were starting to walk offstage, Danny came up to us and said, "Well, boys, it looks like you have a decent crowd waiting in line outside. You must have done some good promoting. Have a good show, guys, and I will be meeting with you later." I had a bad feeling that everyone is going to be pissed about the free-beer trick.

We took the stage as they were letting people in at the door. The place began to fill up fast, and I mean fast. Over half of them immediately flooded the bar. Some came down to the floor in front of the stage. We were just about to start our first song when I looked over and could see all kinds of commotion starting at the bar. I looked over at Sebastian and the guys and said, "Oh no, guys, are you seeing what I am seeing?"

Sebastian said, "Yes, I do, and we predicted this would happen, so let's get ready to save grace before we get thrown off stage. All right, boys, on my count, one, two, one, two, three!"

I started playing the opening riff to one of our originals. Sebastian screamed into the microphone, "Are you ready, Dino's?"

Then, Marc came slamming down on to his cymbals, and Anthony was tearing the bass up. We were off to a hell of a start. About a minute into the song, I could see the bartenders raising their hands because they were confused. There was some serious arguing going on at the bar. Danny came running from across the place with some security guards. The place was loud and about to be torn apart. I tried my best to stay focused on the song, but I couldn't stop looking over at the bar. Then, a customer pulled out one of our flyers, and Danny pulled it from his hands. I knew he saw the free beer because he whipped his head over toward our direction and gave us the death stare. Shit was about to go down as he came running over to the side of the stage. He signaled Pat to kill the sound, and so he did. Danny yelled from the side of the stage, "You fucking assholes, you think this is a way to get people to your shows. What in the hell is this shit!" He pointed to the "free beer" on the flyer and then followed up with, "I want you all to get the hell off my stage and out of my bar!"

Sebastian threw his microphone stand to the floor and yelled right back, "Read the flyer again, dickhead! It says we got a new single called 'Free Beer,' you dumb ass!"

Danny looked back at the banner closely, and then Sebastian said, "Now have Pat bring the sound back, and we will save this place from being destroyed!"

Danny yelled back, "All right, you have sixty seconds to straighten this out, and you better keep them in here, or I will personally make sure my security team fucks you boys up!" Danny went over to Pat and had him bring the sound back. Sebastian picked the microphone stand back up and said, "Hey, everyone, listen up! I know most of you have seen our flyer that said 'free beer,' but we want you to know that is one of our songs that we wrote. We are sorry for the confusion."

The people started booing and throwing stuff at us. They were flipping us off and cursing. We might have made a really bad decision, but we only had a few more seconds. Many people started to head for the exit when Sebastian whispered in my ear what song to start. Then he yelled into the mic, "Fuck this, you ready boys, one, a one two three four!" I started to play the opening riff to "Welcome to the Jungle" by Guns N' Roses. The crowd had a lot of built-up rage, so we gave them something they would recognize. Pat, the sound guy, had everything dialed in right. They finally quit throwing things at us and started listening. When Sebastian came in with his amazing vocals, the place just went berserk. He sang, "Welcome to the jungle, we got fun and games. We got everything you want, honey, we know the names. We are the people that can find whatever you may need. If you got the money, honey, we got your disease!"

Everybody and their brother started singing the chorus out loud. "In the jungle, welcome to the jungle, watch it bring you to your knees. I wanna watch you bleed!" The people who were in the middle of leaving stopped and turned around. Danny's face was priceless. He was in total shock that people were staying. The four of us were giving it everything we had. All that practicing was paying off. Then the guitar solo part came in, and I slid to my knees and bent the hell out of those strings. My adrenaline was pumping, and I fed off the crowd's intensity. Sweat was pouring down my face from how hot those par can lights got. They were nice for lighting the stage, but it felt like I was playing in the middle of the African desert. Marc was whipping his hair back and forth from behind the drum set. He would do these awesome tricks with his drum sticks. Sebastian ran back and forth on that stage and was singing his heart out. I provided backup vocals for him. The ladies were going crazy for Sebastian. I mean he really knew how to work it.

After that song was over, the crowd cheered so loud I couldn't even think. They loved rock 'n' roll, and the night was just getting started. In between covers, we would play our originals. In the middle of the set, Sebastian stepped to the mic and said, "You guys, kick ass! I want you to know that after we are done playing, I am bringing the party back to my place, and you all are invited!" The crowd cheered even louder. This was a good sign that we were doing something right on this stage. Then he said, "I want to introduce you to the guys. On the drums is Marc Allenhart! This man calls his drum kit Sally, and he bangs her almost every night!" Marc put his head down because he was embarrassed, but the crowd was eating it up. Then he stood up from behind the kit and bowed to the crowd. Sebastian followed up with, "On the bass, you have Anthony Wildman Martini! Ladies, this man is one who makes all the rumble in the jungle with his instrument." Anthony's goofy ass stepped to the mic and said, "That's right, I invented the vibrator." He then winked at four girls standing near the stage, but they were not having it. Sebastian then said, "Ladies and gentleman, on lead guitar, David Taylor! He is the next Eddie Van Halen. So make some noise, Dino's!" The crowd clapped and cheered, and at that moment, I felt a tight bond with these guys. Since the crowd was so drunk and having a good time, we cut out playing the "Free Beer" song because we knew if we brought it back out, they would probably burn the place to the ground.

CHAPTER 14

Escape

Once the show ended, we had all kinds of people coming up to us wanting autographs and pictures. They thought we were rock stars. About ten people brought us drinks. The party was just about to start, and I wasn't complaining about free drinks. I've never had this much fun before. After we got outside and started packing the trailer, Danny came out back to speak with us. He said, "So I want to say that was one hell of a show, and you guys pulled it off. I wanted to kick you guys in the head, but you turned a near disaster into success. I owe you guys an opening slot for a bigger band, and I will pay you like we agreed."

"Thanks, Danny," Sebastian said.

Danny turned and looked at me, "Nice guitar playing, kid, I underestimated all of you. You guys definitely have potential to kick some major ass."

I said, "Thanks, Danny, but I couldn't thank these guys enough for giving me the opportunity to play with them."

"Well, boys, I know you're ready to get out of here, so I am going to give you fifty dollars. Now go party, and once I check the schedule, I will give you guys a call."

We packed up the trailer and headed to the nearest gas station to get beer. After we got to Sebastian's place, about fifty people showed up. His house couldn't even hold fifteen people let alone fifty. It was a mixture of guys and girls. Sebastian yelled, "Come on in, we got room!" We just kept all the gear in the trailer, so it wouldn't get damaged. The girls who were showing up were so sexy. They were barely wearing anything. They all brought their own alcohol. Anthony and Marc held a competition to who could outdrink each other. I thought that was retarded because their night was going to end early. Sebastian brought me in to the kitchen and said, "I got something special for you, rock star."

"Oh, really, what is that?" I replied.

He reached into a cabinet and grabbed his favorite bottle of whiskey. He grabbed two shot glasses and poured us a drink. He said, "Drink up, my man, you deserve it."

"Thanks, you too."

"You are family now, David. I know you have been through a lot, and the guys are really proud of you. This is just the beginning of great things to come."

I never had a real family growing up, so that meant a lot to me when he said that. We toasted and took a drink. Sebastian slammed his shot glass down and yelled, "Now let's party!"

We partied like it was 1960. Shortly after, Anthony came up to me completely wasted and mumbled, "Hey, man, you see those two girls in the corner looking at us?"

I looked over to the corner of the room and saw two gorgeous girls. One had black hair, and the other was blonde. I looked at them, and they turned and giggled at each other. I replied to Anthony, "Yes, I see them, and what about them?"

"They like us, man, and I am going to bang the blonde one, or at least I am going to try. If I were you, I would go for the other one," he said.

"The last time you guys told me that, I ended up with the town whore."

"Hey, we're brothers now, and we are going to do plenty of dumb shit. I'm just saying don't let her get lonely."

I looked at him, "I thought you had a girlfriend."

He burped in my face as he replied, "I have one almost every other day, brother."

"You're such a whore, but if you think you got a chance, go get it." He then walked over to the blond girl, and then all I saw was him taking her hand, and they went into Sebastian's room. I stood there for a minute and was thinking damn he is good. The other girl just stood there making it look like she wasn't trying to look at me. Then Sebastian came up to me with his arms around two girls holding a beer. He said to me, "Hey, man, I am heading back to my room for the night with these two beautiful girls. Why don't you go talk to that girl and trust me it won't be an Erica moment."

"I am, and did you know that Anthony is back there with her friend?" I said.

He replied, "It's all good, and you ready, ladies?" They giggled as they went back there with Sebastian. That was going to be one hell of an orgy.

Everyone was so damn drunk, including me. I walked over to speak to that girl. The song "Lay It On the Line" by Triumph was playing on the radio in the background. She was wearing black shorts and had a Nirvana tank top. I saw Marc passed out on the couch with one hand holding a beer and the other in his pants. I guess Anthony won the drinking battle. I said to the girl, "Hi, my name is David, what's yours?"

She replied bashfully, "My name is April. You guys were really good tonight, and I enjoyed your show."

"Thank you and thanks for coming to the party."

"Yeah your welcome, my friend wanted to come because she has a thing for your bass player, and as you can see, they are getting busy."

"Yeah I would say so, can I get you a drink?"

"I would like that, thank you."

I went and grabbed a drink and said, "So you don't have a boyfriend nearby that I need to watch out for?"

"No, but I am glad you came over because this guy across from us keeps staring at me," she said.

I looked across the room at him, and he wasn't even trying to hide it. He was standing about 6'2" and probably in his late forties with tattoos up and down both arms. I looked back at her and said, "How about I tell him you're with me, and that should end that."

"Please do, he is kinda creeping me out," April pleaded.

I walked over to this guy and said, "Hey, man, that's my girl over there, and she's a little weirded out because you keep staring at her. So I am asking nicely if you could knock it off."

He crossed his arms and said, "So just because you guys are in a band, you could get any girl you want? Fuck you, and what are you going to do about it, bitch?"

This guy just literally pissed me off, and it was clear he had a thing for her, and so I said, "I am going to knock you the hell out."

Then out of nowhere, he reached out and grabbed me by my shirt and swung at me. Knocked me back into the wall so I swung back at him. People in the room yelled, "Fight!"

Marc immediately jumped up off the couch and yelled, "Oh, hell no!" He came rushing over to protect me, and then the guy's friend tackled Marc. They were wrestling on the ground and throwing punches. April ran to the back to get Sebastian and Anthony. As she was pounding on the door and screaming about the fight, Anthony and Sebastian came running out in their underwear. Sebastian tackled the guy I was fighting, and Anthony started kicking the other guy who was wrestling Marc. Bottles of beer were flying, and people were cheering it on. Sebastian yelled, "I invite you fuckers back to my place, and this is how we get treated. You attack my guitar player and drummer!"

Bodies were being tossed every which direction. All I could see was fists a-flying. Then Marc screamed, "Now this dude is biting me!"

I glanced over and saw someone biting Marc on the arm. It was actually kinda of funny to hear him yell that. Marc was able to get to his feet because of the choke hold Anthony had on the guy. The girls were trying to stop it but were getting nowhere. The fight started to spill out into the front yard. In the distance, you could hear some girl talking to a dispatcher. She yelled, "Nine one one, yes, please send help to 420 South Ridge Avenue. These guys are attacking my friends, and we need your help. Hurry, please hurry!"

This party was about to come to a crashing end. It was two thirty in the morning, and everyone within a mile radius could hear all the commotion. Sebastian had the one guy in a full nelson hold and yelled to me, "Hit him as hard as you can, David!" I swung as hard as I could, nailing him in the jaw.

Sebastian yelled, "Hell, yeah, man!" Then we heard the police sirens coming. Someone shouted, "Oh shit, scatter, it's the 5-0!" Everyone started to run once they heard the police was on the way. The guys we were fighting ran faster than illegal Mexicans running from INS. Just before the police arrived, I looked at Sebastian and said, "Hey, man, the police, you know what will happen once they look me up."

"Go, David, go, I will take care of the police."

"Thanks, buddy, I owe you one."

"No problem, man, now go, and I will call you soon."

I took off running behind the house. There was a dark alley that would lead me back to the music store. Once I got into the alley, April came running up behind and said, "Hey, where you going?"

I was walking away from her and grunted, "I am walking home."

"Why won't you tell the police what happened?"

"Because I just can't, it's a long story," I said.

She reached out and grabbed my arm, "Please let me take you home."

I was still fired up about the fight, and I was kinda being a jerk to her. I stopped, turned around, and said, "What do you want from me?"

"That was a brave thing you did for me, so at least, will you let me take you home?" April replied.

I paused for a second and finally calmed down. I said, "OK, that's fine, where's your car?"

"Parked a couple of houses down from the party. Just follow my lead, and don't worry about the police, I got this."

I followed April to her car, and I could see the police talking to Sebastian in the distance. She was parked far enough down that they weren't going to know anything. We got into her little Toyota Camry. As we were driving away, I said to her, "Thank you for taking me home, and I am sorry if I came off as a jerk back there in the alley. I was upset and still stewing about him laying his hands on me."

She said, "Oh, well, screw him, you got a few good punches in, and your buddies crack me up."

"How is that?"

"They came out fighting in their underwear."

We both started laughing, and then I said, "Yeah, you don't see that every day. We are a band of brothers, and we stick together."

"Yeah, I could tell, and that's a good thing. I think you guys are great, and I wish you all the best of luck."

"Thank you, and just drop me off right here behind the music store."

We pulled up behind the store, and I thanked her one more time. Then she asked, "So I don't mean to be nosy, but is this where you live?"

"Yeah, for now until I get back on my feet. I've been through a lot the past few years."

"It's all good. I have been in similar situations, but I always say no matter how bad you have it, someone else out there has it worse."

I glanced at her. "Well, if that ain't true."

She whimpered, "Oh, hun, hold still, your lip is bleeding. Let me get you something to wipe it off with." She reached into her purse and grabbed a tissue. She told me not to move. As she was wiping the blood off, she leaned in a little bit closer to me. I did the same, and we stared into each other's eyes for a second, and then we kissed. Her lips were soft, and she smelled like cherry blossoms. We held it out for a good five seconds, and then she leaned back and said, "I like you, David, I really do."

"I like you too, but the last girl I liked ended up screwing me over."

She followed up with, "Well, I want you to know that unlike my friend, I am not a groupie. I just don't sleep around like she does. There is something about you that I find very attractive."

My whole perspective of her changed after that. I thought she was only interested in sex, but it looks like I might be wrong this time. I said back to her, "So if I ask you out, you promise you're not going to bail on me unless I deserve it?"

"If you ask me out on a date, I will promise you that."

I was quick to respond, "OK, April, will you go out with me?"

"Of course, I will."

It was very awkward and unique how this all panned out especially after the show. I trusted that she would be a woman of her word. Plus, I was a sucker for dark-haired girls. She then said, "Here is my number, so I better be receiving a call soon." She winked at me after that.

"How about instead of me calling you, we go out Friday night? The only downfall is that I don't have a car, so if you could pick me up, that would be great," I suggested.

She smiled and followed up with, "Sounds wonderful, now go, and get some rest, rock star, you deserve it."

I waved as she drove away, and I headed to bed.

CHAPTER 15

The Memory Remains

Friday came around, and it was time. April pulled up behind the store around 6:30 PM. She honked her horn, and I came running up the steps. I was dressed up decently, and as soon as I opened the door, I saw her wearing a short black leather skirt with a tight shirt saying Pearl Jam. She almost gave me a semi. I said, "Wow, you look sexy."

"Thanks and you look like a sexy rock star yourself."

I chuckled as I said, "Thanks and since you're driving, where would you like to go?"

"I am not into that fancy shit, so why don't we go get some ice cream, and I know this great spot on top of a mountain that overlooks the town."

"That sounds amazing, let's do it," I said.

"It will be peaceful and quiet," she mentioned as we pulled into a Dairy Queen drive-through and ordered some ice cream. While we were waiting behind a few cars, I said to her, "I can pay for it."

"No, that's OK, darling, I got it."

"I feel bad, I should be the one buying, I am the one who asked you out," I replied.

"It's OK, you buy next time."

In my mind, I was thinking that maybe she was taking me out instead.

It was about a couple hours from sunset. We drove for a good minute up this dirt road that was surrounded by trees. You could see the sun shining through the trees and lighting the dirt road up. Right as we got to the top of the hill, it opened up, and you could see the entire town and the Ohio River. It was like a beautiful scene out of a romance movie. She parked her car close to the edge and got out a blanket for us to sit on. We sat down and began to eat our ice cream and start our conversation.

"So David, what brought you to Chesapeake?" April asked.

"I was tired of things and was looking for a fresh, new start. How did you know I was new here?"

"I know a little more than you think, David. You see I grew up with Sebastian, and so I spoke to him at the party about you."

"Oh, great, what all did he tell you?"

She answered, "He didn't say much, trust me it was like he was protecting you. He did say you were a good guy, just had some trouble growing up, and that's pretty much all he said. Sebastian knew that I liked you, and that's why I asked."

I said with shame, "I don't know why you would like me. I live in the basement of a music store and don't even have a car. I have come a long way from my past though."

April reached over and grabbed my hand and said, "You're different from the rest of those guys, and I see that. You can tell me, I promise your word is safe with me."

I paused for a second and took a breath and stared over the town. I said, "I was locked up for four years. I had a rough life growing up with no real parents. I ran around with the wrong crowd, and that led me into a life of drugs at a young age. I had an uncontrollable ego that led me straight to prison. There were things that happened to me in prison that changed me. I saw horrible things, and sometimes it's hard to sleep at night. I learned how to play music in there, and that was my way of surviving. Plus, there was a man who I need to go back and visit."

"Who is this man?" April asked.

"A man who I think is the reason why I am not dead. I plan on going back to see him soon."

"What was his name?"

"His name was John. After prison, I drifted here with my book bag and guitar. I slept under a bridge for a few days." I pointed in the direction of where the bridge was. "I met Sebastian at Dino's when they held the open jam. Then I met Dick, and he helped me keep a roof over my head until I get back on my feet. Now I'm here, and I don't have any complaints because I believe that things happen for a reason."

April had the look of shock on her face as she replied, "I am so sorry to hear that, but I know that you will go far with these guys. I also want to meet this John fellow. He sounds like a decent guy."

April talked about her story, "I had some problems growing up, nothing like what you've been through."

"What happened?" I asked.

She went on to explain, "My dad left me and my mom when I was six. I didn't have any brothers or sisters, so my mom raised me to be strong and independent. She taught me how to deal with assholes that just want to get into my pants. I know if I ever run into my dad, I would break his fucking jaw."

I said, "Do you know exactly why he left your mom and you?"

"Mom says that he just took off with another woman. Left without a trace, but it's whatever now, I am a grown woman, and I can take care of myself. I am a manager at the carry-out store not far from here. I deal with all kinds of crap each day. I really want to be a crime scene investigator. I don't know what it is about that, but it just seems like fun, plus I want to catch bad guys."

"I noticed that about you, you seem very independent. You also strike me as a leader and a problem solver."

She smiled. "Aww, thank you, you're so sweet. What are you doing tonight?"

"After this, not a damn thing. Maybe practice on my guitar for a few hours at my place until I pass out. Why, what's up?"

"How about you come stay at my place? I got a nice apartment not far from here. I know that can't be the most comfortable place to stay."

I replied, "Oh really, that is awesome of you. I don't think it would hurt anything, plus Dick might be getting tired of me staying down there. He hasn't said anything yet, but I'm sure he is getting ready to soon."

The sun was almost gone, and it was starting to get dark. I went ahead and threw the blanket in the back seat. As I was getting ready to shut the back passenger door, I felt a hand grab the door. I turned around, and there stood April inches away staring at me with this sexual look. She closed the car door and pushed me up against it. I said, "Are you OK?"

"Yeah, I am, now shut up and kiss me," she replied.

I slowly grabbed her by the back of her head and pulled her close. We kissed and we kissed, and as we were kissing, she reached for the door handle. I moved away from the door, and she opened it and pushed me into the back seat. She climbed on top of me all sexy-like and kissed me some more. I would stick my tongue in her mouth, and I could feel her sucking on it. The feeling I had with this girl was strong, and I am pretty sure she was feeling the same way. She took my shirt off and started kissing my chest. April took her shirt off and said, "You OK, darling?"

I whispered softly, "Oh, yeah, you're just so damn beautiful. How did a lucky guy like me end up meeting such a sexy girl like you?"

She whispered back, "Thank you, darling, now sshh and relax, I will take care of you."

In the background, you could hear the song "Wonderful Tonight" by Eric Clapton. We made love in the back seat of that car for a good hour. The windows were so steamed up, and the shocks in that car definitely got a workout. Once we were finished, April stepped out to smoke a cigarette. She spoke to me from outside the car, "That was amazing, David, you sure got the moves, and I can tell you have had practice."

I replied jokingly, "Oh, yeah, that's why the ladies call me a sex god."

She didn't find it that funny. "Well, rock star, it's getting dark, you about ready to go?"

"I am ready when you are," I answered.

We both got up front and headed back to her place.

She pulled up to this apartment complex about a mile from Dino's. Her place was very girly, but you could tell she liked her rock music. The place was just a one-bedroom apartment. The kitchen was small, but the living room was bigger. She had a glass coffee table and a two-piece couch set with a recliner. Most of her decorations were pink because that was her favorite color. Another thing she really enjoyed was movies. She had a big selection of movies on VHS.

"Please have a seat on the couch and make yourself at home. Would you like a soda or a beer?"

"A Bud Light would be fine," I replied.

As she was getting us a beer, she asked me to pick out a movie. I went over to her movie shelf and started browsing. Her movies were all in alphabetical order. I never watched many movies as a kid so I was clueless on what to pick. She walks up to me and hands me my beer and says, "Oh, having trouble finding a movie?" I replied, "Yeah, there are so many to choose from, and I don't know what's good or not."

"Here let me help you. You like action or horror?"

"I can go for a good horror movie," I said.

She reaches into the shelf and grabs Stephen King's *Silver Bullet.* She says, "I think you will like this, it's about a werewolf who terrorizes this small town."

"That sounds cool, let's go with that one." I said as I popped in the movie, and we cuddled up on the couch. I had never seen this movie before, and she said it was a classic. In the opening scene, a railroad worker was walking along some railroad tracks. He spots wolf prints in the dirt, and you could hear the werewolf getting closer. He attacks the worker and knocks his head clean off his shoulders. It is hard to get scared when you know what's about to happen. The music in a lot of movies can really give the scene away. I liked the man who composed the main theme track to the movie. Now that was creepy. I'm sure if I saw it when it first came out, I would have shit my pants. As we were watching, April would get scared every time he attacks. She would snuggle up closer and closer. We were about halfway into the movie when she started rubbing my crotch under the blanket. She went from being scared to being horny. It was very hard to focus on the movie, and so I just turned my head, and we starting making out again. She muted the movie, and we went at it again. I didn't have a lot of juice left, but I was still going strong. It started on the couch then went to the floor and eventually ended up in her bedroom. The sex was so good, I don't think of any man who could resist. I was able to get another load out, and that damn near made me pass out. She rolled over from being on top of me and said, "Holy shit, David, I didn't think you had any left."

"I didn't think I had any either, but I'm not complaining," I said.

She mentioned, breathing heavily, "I normally don't sleep with guys on the first date, but there is an exception with you."

"I wasn't going to turn it down, but why didn't you?"

"I got a certain feeling with you. Something I never felt before. It's complicated and hard to explain, but that's why."

We lay there for a few seconds while she ran her fingers up and down on my chest. Then I heard someone knocking at the door. "I think someone's at the door, babe," I muttered.

We paused for a second, and she yelled, "Who is it?"

They wouldn't answer back, but just kept knocking. So April got out of bed and threw on some sweatpants and a shirt. As she started opening the door, I heard a scream for help. I jumped up out of bed and headed toward her screams. My heart was racing, and fear was sinking in. As soon as I came around the corner, I saw four black thugs. One was on top of her, holding her down. I lunged at them yelling, "Get your fucking hands off her!"

One of the men said, "What you going to do about it, bitch?"

The other three men attacked me, and our fists were flying. It was a three-on-one battle, and I lost. I was knocked to the ground. I was lying on my belly, and I could see April on her back reaching for my hand. She yelled, "David! Help me!"

They had me held down tight. I yelled, "Leave her alone! I swear I am going to kill all of you."

The leader of the group leaned over and said to April, "Look over at him, bitch, and watch because you're next!"

She cried out, "What are you going to do to us?"

I was doing my best to break free, but I couldn't move or see what they were doing behind me. I yelled, "Oh, babe, what are they about to do?" She was crying so hard and trying to tell them to stop. I then felt a tight pressure in my rear end. I started hearing noises faintly in the distance saying, "David, damn it, David, wake up!" My body was being shook excessively. I woke up, and April was standing in front of me with her hands on my shoulders. She was saying, "David, baby, are you OK?"

I was panting heavily as I said, "I'm fine, I'm fine, I just had a bad dream." The movie credits were rolling on the TV as she said, "Oh, I can tell, I was getting worried there for a second because you wouldn't wake up. I thought Freddy Krueger was after you."

I realized at that moment that I had fell asleep on the couch after the movie was over, and I was having flashbacks in my dreams. I dreamed our entire sex scene, and my dream took me back to that day in prison. A day I never want to relive. April asked me, "What was your dream about, darling?"

I wouldn't tell her, so I said it was about the movie.

She replied and was kinda making fun of me, "Oh, poor baby gets nightmares after watching scary movies."

"Yeah, yeah, so what?"

April yawned and said, "I don't know about you, darling, but I am getting tired, but I am going to take a shower real quick."

"How about I join you? And we both call it a night."

She stood up and walked over to the bathroom. She slowly took her pants off at the door entrance, turned to me slowly, and said, "Of course, you can, baby, now come join me." I stood behind her in the shower and put my arms around her while kissing her on the neck. We made slow love and crashed hard for the night.

CHAPTER 16

Creeping Death

It's been well over a year since I saw John. In the fall of 1999, I decided to take a trip back to Oaksville State Penitentiary. I wanted to know how John was doing. When I got there, I pulled up to the main gate, and a guard came out from his station. He came up to the driver side window and said, "Can I help you?"

"I am here to visit an inmate."

"Sorry, buddy, but visiting hours are over." The guard stared at me for a second with this funny look on his face and said, "Wait a minute, you look familiar. You were locked up here about a couple of years ago. You play music, don't you?"

"Yes, sir, that was me."

"Well, why the hell would you want to come back here and visit?"

I then looked through the front window at the facility as I answered, "The man who helped believe in my music is locked up in there."

The guard said, "OK, let me see what I can do, just give me a second."

I waited in the car for a few minutes. Then the gate started to open. He waved me through and showed me where to park. Once I got out, I headed for the entrance. Memories were running through my head like a disease, and most of them were bad. I signed in at the front desk, and the lady gave me a visitor badge. Rex, the old guard, came up to me and said, "Welcome back to Oaksville, I guess I won't be escorting you to a cell."

"I am afraid not, Rex, but I am here to see John, is he available?" I asked.

"Yeah, right this way."

We both walked down the hall to the visitors' room. In this room, they had stools lined up in front of a long glass window. The glass was in sections and attached to it was a phone for communication on both sides. I never had any visitors, so I never knew this room existed. Rex said, "Take a seat anywhere, and John will be in."

I sat on the stool and waited a couple minutes. Then I heard a door open from the other side, and here came John with a big smile on his face. His face was skinny, and it looked like he had lost some weight. Still wearing that orange jumpsuit, he sat down across from me, and we both picked up the phones to speak.

"David, it's good to see you, thanks for coming back to see me. How you been?"

"Things have been great, John, and it's good to see you're still going strong."

"Yeah, same shit, different day. The only thing that sucks is I'm getting old. So please fill me in, I want to know what's happened since you left here."

I said, "Oh, where do I start? After I got out, I went back home and realized that there was nothing there for me, so I started looking for a fresh, new start. I drifted from one town to the next and finally came across this town called Chesapeake. It's about three hours down south from here. I ended up living under a bridge because I had nowhere to stay."

"Oh, man, I don't want to hear bad news," John blurted.

I continued, "Hold on, man, it gets better, a lot better. I met a music store owner who went by the name of Dick Newman. I kinda told him my story, and he gave me a place to crash temporarily. Oh, I forgot to tell you, you know that guitar that the warden gave me right before I left?"

"Yeah, the acoustic you learned on, what about it?"

"A couple of lowlifes stole it from me when I was living under that bridge."

"Are you serious, please tell me you got it back."

"I did, the dumb ass tried to sell it to Dick at the music store."

John started laughing and said, "Wow, what a retard, but that is good news for you, go on tell me more."

"I got it back, and I met a great lead singer at this place called Dino's Bar 'n' Grill. We ended up forming a band with two other members that he used to know. They love my guitar playing, and our first show was killer."

"Damn, that is great to hear. You meet a girl yet?" he asked.

"Yes, I did, and her name is April, and we have been dating for a while now. She was going to come, but there was an issue at her work, so she couldn't. She has been taking care of me while I chase this dream with the guys."

After telling him all this good news, I could tell that there was something on John's mind, so I said, "What's wrong, John, something is on your mind, I can tell?"

He paused for a second and put his hand over his mouth to cover his cough. Once he pulled his hand away, I saw blood and said, "John, you're coughing up blood, what the hell's going on?"

He said with shame, "I'm dying, David, and the doctor says the cancer has spread pretty far. He thinks I only have a couple more years until I check out."

I just stared at him with this depressed look and said, "Oh, damn it, I didn't need to hear that, you should be a free man in the first place. If there is anything I can do for you, just let me know."

"Don't worry about it, buddy, I will be fine, and thanks, I did talk to the warden, and he said that if it gets worse, he will release me so I can die a free man. He mentioned something about compassionate release, but that's up in the air with him. I've been here so long, I don't even know if I could cope with the outside world, even if it's only a couple months. I have been on his good list for a while, but I can't hold my breath on it."

"You give me a call if that happens, and we will meet up," I demanded.

"You're damn right I will, I want to see you and your band play live."

"Backstage passes for you if we get famous," I said.

Rex stepped in and said time was almost up.

"Well, John, it was good seeing you again, and I hope the warden lets you out soon."

"It was good seeing you, David, don't worry about me. I will be fine. I wish the best of luck with the band and your girl, and remember don't give up."

We both hung up the phones, and it was time for me to go.

When I got back, I opened the door and saw April pacing back and forth in the living room. I said, "Hey, babe, I am back, are you OK?"

"I'm fine, just had a rough day."

"You sure you're OK? You're acting funny."

She snapped with a little anger, "I said I'm fine! Go play your guitar or something." Something weird was going on with her. My best bet was to leave her alone for a few minutes, and maybe she will tell me.

"OK, I got to use the bathroom, so I will leave you alone." I went to the bathroom to take a dump, and as I was sitting there reading my guitar magazine, I looked over and saw what looked like a test kit in the trash can. I leaned over to grab it, and the box said pregnancy test. I didn't know what to think or how to approach her about this. My mind started racing about 1,000 miles per hour. I started sweating profusely. I wasn't ready to be a father nor did I make enough to support a baby. I put the box back in the trash, and when I was finished, I approached her in the living room. I said, "Babe, is there something you would like to talk about?"

She replied nervously, "No, I'm fine, I told you."

I started to get a little frustrated because I knew she was lying, "No, you're not fine, I know you're lying."

After pacing, she sat down on the couch and started crying. I sat down next to her and rubbed her back. She continued to cry as she tried to speak, "I'm sorry, but there is something you need to know."

"You can tell me," I said.

"If I do, you promise not to freak out on me?"

"I promise, babe, now what is it?" I knew exactly what was about to come out of her mouth but wasn't expecting some of the things she was about to say.

"David, I'm pregnant. I'm scared to death because I am not ready to be a mother. You're going to have to get a full-time job and quit your band."

I fired right back in my defense, "Calm down, and don't be saying shit like that. I'm not quitting my band, so don't try to tell me how it's going to be. We are in this together, so please calm down!"

She fired back at me, "No, don't tell me to calm down, I'm fucking pregnant and scared! I might have to get an abortion."

I yelled, "Shut up! Shut the fuck up! I don't want to hear that word. I understand you're upset, and so am I. I love you, April, and we will be just fine, I promise. Wasn't it you who told me no matter how bad it is, someone else has it worse?" I did my best to calm her down and get her to stop crying. It took about an hour of talking to get her to calm down. We both had to suck it and accept the fact that we were going to be parents.

CHAPTER 17

The House Waylon Built

The next practice we had, Sebastian brought a guy in named Waylon Boise. He was a short guy with a scruffy beard. He looked like a guy you wouldn't want to pick a fight with. Anthony and I were sitting on the couch while Marc was doing some tune-up work on his drums. Sebastian said, "Guys, I want you to meet Waylon. He has a few things he would like to share with us."

After we all introduced ourselves, Sebastian said, "OK, now that's all done, what do you have to offer?"

Waylon went on to explain, "Well, guys, I saw your show over at Dino's, and I was very impressed. You guys have a lot of potential, and I think I might be able to help get you where you need to be."

The rest of us looked over at each other, and we're nodding our heads up and down.

"OK, you have our attention." Sebastian said.

He continued, "I want to tell you a little bit about me and my background before I get into all the details. I used to work for a four-piece band out of the Columbus area. I spent a lot of time with them in the recording studio and on set of their music videos. I learned a lot about the business side of music and how things operated. I was older than those guys, so I got tired and worn-out from traveling around with them so I moved down south here to open up a small recording studio. My goal is to help young inspiring musicians get demo recordings. It's up to them after that if they want to take it to the next level. I have a decent amount of connections to producers and agents. So what I am trying to get at is that I think you guys can make it. I've seen a lot of bands come and go in my days, but I saw how hungry you guys were on that stage, and you reminded me of those boys."

"What was the name of the band?" I asked.

"Cross Solder, pronounced like Saw Der. However, I would like to record your first demo. So this is my deal for you, guys. For a small price, I will record your demo, and then I will personally take it to the record label that worked with that band. I can't promise you anything, but if they do accept you, you will be working with this amazing producer. His name is Joe Collins, and he has worked with some of the world's biggest artists including Ted Nugent, Steve Vai, and members of Kiss."

I looked over at Marc, and his eyes got huge. Remember, he was a huge Kiss fan, and so I replied, "Hell, yeah, you can record our demo and take it to him!"

Waylon said, "I know once Joe hears your demo, he will record you. You guys will be one big step closer to achieving your goals as a band."

I said to the guys, "Well, guys, what do we have to lose?"

We all agreed with each other.

Then, Waylon said, "If you don't have much going on, why don't you guys follow me over to my studio and check it out?"

We were all excited, but Marc was acting like a child in the candy store. Sebastian looked at me and Anthony, "You guys want to go check this studio out?"

The three of us didn't reply. We just started heading outside to the van. Sebastian looks at Waylon and says, "I guess that answers my question."

We were just going to follow Waylon in his little red pickup truck. It was about a five-mile drive from our practice spot. We loaded up, and on our way, we went. We pulled into this driveway that led to this trailer home. As all of us were getting out of the van, Waylon said, "Yeah, I know it's not what you expected, but wait until we get inside."

He unlocks the door, and the first room on the other side of the door was the control room. There was a computer hooked up to his twenty-four-channel mixing board. It said Mackie on the top right corner of the board. He had a couple couches along the back side of the wall. Posters of his favorite bands were hanging up along with naked Playboy models. The carpet was filthy from everyone tracking back and forth on it. There was a window that looked from the control room into the main room that probably was a living room at one time. In the main room, there were cables and all kinds of microphones lying around. The trash cans were full of empty beer cans from the band before. He had a spot along the back side for the drums. The windows in the room were covered with black curtains, so no one could look in. The walls had this rubber foam for sound damping. A couple Marshall cabinets for guitar recordings were in the same room along with an Ampeg bass cabinet. In the direct center of the room was the stand for the singer to stand and record. I thought this place was really cool. It was a trailer home completely flip-flopped into a studio.

Waylon said, "It's not the best studio in the world, but for live demo recording, it gets the job done."

"It's perfect for what we need to do." Sebastian added.

"Yeah, dude, some of the greatest artists come from studios like this," Anthony added.

"Thanks, guys, and like I said, this will help you get on your feet and get people listening to you. We are going to capture the intensity that I got from the stage that night, and then we can go from there."

"OK, how much will it cost us to come in and record?" Sebastian asked.

"For you guys, I will only charge one hundred dollars for a full ten-hour day, and that should be enough for your demo. If we go over that a little bit, I won't charge you anything."

I said to everyone in the room, "Damn, that's not a bad deal at all for that amount of time."

"Well, boys, when you want to get in here?" Sebastian asked.

"I am pretty open all next week, so whatever you guys decide, I am good with," Waylon mentioned.

"I am ready right now!" Marc shouted.

"Oh, Marc, I know you're ready, so let's get our asses in here Friday at 10:00 am. Is that cool with all of you?"

Anthony, Marc, and I all agreed that Friday was the day. We had the tunes and attitude to make this happen.

When Friday came around, we loaded up our equipment in the van and headed to the studio. Anthony brought his handheld camera for video recording.

"What's that for, Anthony?" I asked.

"Are you retarded, dude? It's the beginning of our journey. It's a chapter in our band life that I would like to relive, plus people would want to see this footage someday in the future if we were to become famous."

I replied with a dumb look on my face, "Wow, I am retarded, that makes sense, so film away."

When we arrived, Waylon showed us where to bring the gear in. Marc began to set up his drum kit while Anthony and I plugged into Waylon's gear. Once the drums were up and in tune, Waylon came into the room to hook up the microphones. He placed one in front of the kick drum, one for the high hat, snare, and all of the toms. He had two microphones hanging above to capture the crash cymbals. He had the bass going direct out of the amp head into the mixing board. I was still using the Gibson Les Paul, which was hooked up to the Marshall cab with a microphone in front of it. Once that was all done and the instruments were all tuned up, Waylon went into the control room. He had us wearing these headphones so he could communicate to us, and so that we could hear each other better. He clicked the talk-back button and said, "OK, guys, give me just a second to set up the computer and we will be ready. If you want, guys, there is beer in the kitchen so feel free to drink if that helps."

I put down the guitar for a second and said to the fellows, "You guys want a round before we get started?" They all hollered, "Hell, yeah," and so I went and got us a round of beers.

"OK, guys, I am ready when you are. Do you guys want a click track? If not I can take it off," Waylon asked.

I didn't know much about this recording process, so I let the other guys decide what they wanted to do. Sebastian said, "Since it's a demo, you can take it off."

"OK, that's cool, just give it a big four count before you come in."

"Oh, this is so badass, let's start with the song 'Light It Up,' I am going to click my drum sticks four times and then come in, guys," Marc said.

Click, click, click, click, and then boom, we all came in hard. I was playing these badass power chords, and Anthony's bass was sounding so raunchy. It was awesome because I had everyone's volume adjusted just right in my headset. Sebastian was rocking his head back and forth and came in strong on the vocal mic. He sang, "We're going to light it up tonight! So put your fists in the air and let it all out!" Those were the opening lyrics, and Sebastian was nailing it. I could see Waylon through the glass smiling and singing along as he was mixing the track.

After we ran through the first take, Waylon said, "Oh hell, yeah, boys, that is sounding nasty in here. I want to do another take and adjust a few tones. So let's run that from the top one more time, and we can move on to the next track." We laid down eight demo tracks in just three hours. Waylon looked at us and said, "Damn, you guys know how to rock, and your chemistry is tight. I know that when I get this demo put together, the record label will be very interested. Step in here, boys, and let's listen to what I've captured." We all sat on the couch in the control room and listened to what Waylon captured. We were blown away at the sound quality he was able to produce. Waylon said that it would take a few days to get it all put together, but the hardest part was over. Sebastian turned and said, "Gentlemen, let's have a toast to the next greatest rock band!"

We all raised up our beers and took a huge drink.

CHAPTER 18

Trapped Under Ice

I officially moved out of the music store and in with April to help support the pregnancy. I was going to try and be the best boyfriend I could be, but I didn't realize what was in store for me. She was about four weeks in, and almost every morning, I would hear her throwing up in the bathroom. She scheduled an ultrasound appointment to make sure the baby was OK. She was spotting and cramping throughout the day, and so we were nervous that something might be wrong.

When we arrived at the ob-gyn office, we had to wait for her midwife to see us. The waiting lobby was full of cranky pregnant girls. They had a TV on with pregnancy tips for women and a vending machine in the corner which I thought was hilarious because pregnant women like to eat. I was the only guy in the waiting room, so it felt very awkward. Then, a nurse opened the door and yelled, "April Monroe, the doctor will see you now!"

We both stood up and followed the nurse to the back room. Once we got back there, the nurse weighed her and checked her height. After that, she checked her blood pressure. She told us to step into this small room and wait. In this room was the ultrasound machine. To me, it looked like a futuristic R2-D2 with a computer screen. I started touching it when April whispered loudly, "David, stop! Don't touch that, you might mess it up. Go sit over there on that chair before you get in trouble."

I did what I was told, and about five minutes later, a cute short blond-haired woman with freckles opened the door and said, "Hello, April, my name is Bethany, and I am your midwife. I will be doing your ultrasound today. You say that you have been spotting a lot throughout the day and having some cramps?"

I just sat in the corner and let April do all the talking.

"Yeah, I was starting to get scared that something might be wrong so we decided to schedule an appointment."

Bethany said, "Well, that's very normal in the early stages of pregnancy, but we are going to take a look just in case. What I need you to do now is lie back on the table, and unbutton your pants."

April unbuttoned her pants and lay back on the table.

"Please lift your shirt a little, so I can rub this gel on you. It might be a little cold, so just bear with me." Bethany rubbed this gel that looked like K-Y jelly on her belly. Then out of nowhere, Bethany stood up and went over to lock the door. Bethany turns around and looks me dead in the eye with this sexy look and says, "So, David, I heard you like girl-on-girl action." I was at a loss for words, and then Bethany walks over to April and starts rubbing her vagina. April started moaning, and before I knew it, they were kissing each other. I thought this was very sexy, and I almost bit my lip off. Then I heard April yelling in the distance, "David! Oh, earth to David, hey, David!"

I then realized at that moment I was daydreaming all of this because the midwife was kinda hot. I was having a total perverted moment in my head, and then I looked over and saw April and Bethany staring at me. I said, "I'm sorry, hun, I was in la la land."

Bethany grunted, "Well, now that we have your attention, take a look on the screen." I looked up at the screen, and I saw what looked like a little peanut. I stood up and went over to hold April's hand. She said, "Look, darling, it's our little baby."

Bethany said, "Everything seems to be normal, which is good news. It looks like your due date is August 29. I will print you guys out a picture so you can take it home."

I was excited to become a dad after seeing the ultrasound. As we were wrapping things up, Bethany said to us, "I would recommend, April, that you read the book *What to Expect When You're Expecting*. It has everything in it that will prepare you all the way up to your date of birth. David, there is a section in the book just for men, so if you get a chance, please read it. You can find it at pretty much any bookstore."

"Thanks, we might just go and get it today. Thank you, Bethany, and we will see you again," April said.

After we left the office, we went to the bookstore and got that book. I started reading the men's section that night right before bed, and in the book, it talked about how their hormones will start raging. I had to make sure I just listen to her and let her vent everything. Her feet and face will start to swell. Her emotions will be very vulnerable, so I have to watch everything I say especially about her weight. Fatigue was one of the biggest issues along with certain cravings. It said eventually, her boobs will start to hurt because they are filling with milk. I thought I had a pretty good idea on what to expect, but I was way wrong.

About two months into the pregnancy, I came home from practice, and she flipped out on me. As I came through the front door with my acoustic, I yelled, "Hey, babe, I'm back!"

She came around from the kitchen yelling, "David, we need to have a talk. I need to know what in the hell you are going to do to bring money into this household. I know you love playing music with your band, but I can't afford to take care of this baby on my salary!"

"Baby, trust me, we just got done with our demo, and things are starting to look up. We will be able to get more gigs, and money will start to come in."

I tried to remain calm like the book said as she yelled back, "Oh yeah, well, what if it doesn't happen? You don't have a job, and all you do is sit around and play that fucking guitar! I think it's time for you to grow up and get your ass out there and find a real job!"

At this moment, I was biting my tongue so hard and trying not to yell back. I said calmly, "Listen, hun, I know you got some things on your mind, and I understand, but the band has things lining up. It's also very hard to get a job with a felony on my record."

Then she just kept going, "Oh, great, I should have never got pregnant by an ex-con! I knew I should have dated a lawyer or a doctor."

That was the last straw for me, and then I exploded, "You fucking bitch, I would never have said anything like that to you. I love you, and what in the hell would possess you to say that!"

"You wanna call me a bitch? I am going to teach you a lesson." April then grabbed my acoustic guitar off the couch where I had placed it, and I said, "Babe, what you doing? Please put that down, I am sorry for calling you a bitch."

"You want me to break this? 'Cause I will!" She cried out.

I dropped to my knees and begged her, "Please, baby, don't break it. I am sorry, I take it back. I love you, and let's just sit down and talk about it."

She stood there for a second, breathing heavily with my guitar in the air with both hands on the neck as if she was about to swing a baseball bat. Then, she put the guitar down and started balling her eyes out. I stood up and went over to her and gave her a big hug. She put her head into my shoulder, and the tears flowed like Niagara. I whispered in her ear, "It's going to be OK, I promise."

She lifted her head up and said as she was wiping her tears, "You called me a bitch, and that wasn't very nice." She says that even though she said some crazy mean shit to me. I let that all go and said, "I didn't mean it, baby. I was just being stupid, and I'm sorry."

She continued venting, "I'm getting fat, and I'm afraid you will not want to sleep with me."

I said, "Oh, baby, you're still sexy to me, and you are not fat." I had to lie even though I knew she was getting fat, but that was normal.

Things started to settle down after a while, and everything went back to normal. I was hoping that we wouldn't have any more episodes like this again. Two months later, I made a huge mistake, and it damn near cost me my relationship. April had lost her sex drive this entire time during her pregnancy, and I was having sex withdrawals. I would toss and turn at night because I couldn't get laid. She didn't want nothing to do with sex. It took every ounce of my energy not to want to talk to another girl. So the only solution I had at the time was beating off. I was very secretive about it until she came home early from work one day and caught me beating off in the bedroom to a Playboy magazine. She came into the room and screamed, "Oh my god! Are you serious right now?"

I was sitting on the edge of the bed with the magazine in my lap. I just froze up and had the look of "I'm dead" on my face. I didn't know how to respond. I was busted, and how do you explain that? She continued yelling at me, "Am I not good enough for you? I come home early from work and catch you jerking it to some fake bimbo who you will never sleep with!"

I covered up myself with the blanket and stood up. "I am so sorry, baby, I couldn't resist. We haven't had sex in over four months, and it's killing me!"

She fell to the floor and burst into tears again and said, "I knew you thought I wasn't pretty anymore and so you want to be with another girl."

I replied almost in tears myself, "No, that's not true, I promise you're the only girl I want to be with." I went over to her and tried to put my hand on her shoulder. She stood up immediately with tears running down and yelled, "Get out of my house! Get the fuck out! I don't want to see your face ever again."

I tried to calm her down. "Hun, listen to me, I'm sorry I will get rid of the magazine and never do it again." She smacked the hell out of me and yelled again, "You have ten seconds to get out of my house! I fucking mean it!" I had no choice but to grab a few things and leave. As I was walking out the front door, I stopped and turned around to try and say one more thing, but she just slammed the door on me. I didn't have anywhere to go, so I went out to the corner of the street and just played my acoustic. People in their cars were staring at me as they drove by. I sat out there for two hours until I heard her open the front door. I turned around and looked over my shoulder and saw her poke her head out the door. "David, come in and let's talk."

"OK, I'll be right there." I went back inside and sat down on the couch. She sat next to me and said in a calm voice, "I'm sorry, David, I know I haven't had a sex drive lately, and it's not your fault. I understand that you are sexually frustrated, and that's why you had that magazine."

I just sat and didn't say a word as she continued on. "I love you, and I want you to promise you will never look at that shit again. I can't take it, and I don't need us to be fighting."

I had to respond smartly with my words. "I'm sorry, baby, and I promise you I will never look at the stuff again. I love you, and we got a beautiful baby on the way, and Mommy needs to be stress-free. How about you go lie down and get some rest, and I will help clean the house?"

"Thanks, baby, that sounds nice," she replied.

April went to the bedroom to lie down, and I fell on to the couch taking a huge breath. I had fucked up big time, but luckily, we were able to work it out. I spent the rest of the evening cleaning up the house and tried not to unleash the beast in her again.

CHAPTER **19**

It's Electric

The call came in from Waylon saying the demo was finally finished. We were hoping this was going to be the turning point in our lives. The four of us headed down to the studio to get the CDs. We walked in, and Waylon was sitting at his mixing board. He said as we walked through the door, "Gentlemen, welcome back, I know you guys are going to love the demo, and so here it is." He reached down and picked up a small box.

"Oh hell, yeah, is that our pride and joy?" Sebastian hollered.

Waylon said, "You bet your ass it is. Now I will be trying to contact the record label I was talking about earlier. In the meantime, take these hundred copies, and pass them out to whoever you want.

That should get you guys out there. I will be in touch if I hear anything from the label."

Marc ripped the box from Sebastian's hands, eager to open it and take a copy. Sebastian yanked it back and yelled, "Hey, man, take it easy, everyone in this room will get a copy, so relax."

Sebastian then pulled out a few copies and gave them to all of us. Anthony then came up with a brilliant idea. He said, "Guys, let's all cruise around town and jam this mofo."

Marc responded to him, "You idiot, we all have to get in the car to go home anyway. You didn't think we weren't going to do that in the first place?"

Anthony and Marc always messed with each other. Any chance one could get, they were on it.

We left the studio and drove around town jamming our demo. We had it so loud I thought the speakers were going to blow. As we came to this red light, a couple of ritzy girls pulled up next to us in their convertible. I was sitting in the back with Marc. Sebastian was driving with Anthony up in the front. They pulled up on the passenger side next to Anthony. Marc taps Sebastian on the shoulder and says, "Turn the volume down."

Sebastian then turns the volume down, and Marc taps Anthony on the shoulder saying, "Dude, I dare you to try and give these girls a CD."

Anthony didn't even hesitate. He hangs halfway out the window and yells, "Hey, ladies!"

The two girls turned and looked at Anthony. "I just got out of the recording studio and want you to know that I can make a lot of magic with these two fingers. So what do you say you take one of our CDs, and maybe we will see you at a show?"

The driver replied, "Sorry, buddy, we don't listen to losers like you." Then she flipped him the bird as they drove away. Anthony pulls himself back into the window as we were all laughing at him. He says, "Oh screw them, stupid dykes. I bet all they listen to is fucking Weezer." He looked over at us and continued to rant. "You all think it's funny, huh? I don't see you guys backing me up."

I said to Anthony as I was laughing, "Hey, man, it's all good. There are over 300 million people in this country. Two rich bitch girls aren't worth getting that worked up over."

Sebastian and Marc both agreed with me.

When we got back to Sebastian's house, we all sat around the kitchen table and had a few beers. This is where I started to learn that there was more to music than just rocking out. It was a business, and if we wanted to go far, we had to operate like a business. Sebastian said, "OK, we have a hundred copies, and we all need to figure out how we can get them in the hands of important people. We can't rely on the record label that Waylon was talking about. So I want to hear your ideas on how to better the band."

Marc went first, "I say we just hand them out to whoever will take a copy. You never know how important that person is you're giving it to."

Anthony said, "I don't think that will go very far. We only have these copies and don't have a lot of money to print more."

Marc replied, "You also have to remember this is just a demo and not the final product. So it will only take us so far until we set another goal."

"Guys, I don't know much about this kinda stuff, but remember that show at Dino's?" They all said yes, and I continued. "The reaction we got from the crowd that night was amazing. Imagine how many CDs would have flown out the door that night if we had them?"

Sebastian interrupted and said, "Yeah, he's right, and I see where you are going with this, David. You guys, what did bands like Motley Crue, Van Halen, and Kiss have to do to get their name out there?"

I didn't know what they did, and Anthony says to Sebastian, "OK, smarty pants, what did they do?"

Sebastian went on to explain the perfect strategy, "Those bands took the stage every night with a mission. They would do things on stage that would catch the attention of everyone in the room. Did most of you know that Nikki Sixx would set himself on fire during their set? Shit like that will grab everyone's attention because it is entertaining yet dangerous, but it works. Look at Kiss with all their costume work and makeup. I guarantee you that everyone went home that night and probably told fifty of their friends what they witnessed the night before. We don't have to have the greatest music in the world. Let's face it, we are talented, but let's continue writing songs that are badass to us, and to hell with the rest of the people who don't like it. Those damn bands drew so much attention that the record labels were dying to get their hands on them. They were making money without the labels, and that's why they were wanting them so bad. I have a feeling that in ten to fifteen years, the music industry is going to garbage. It seems to be heading that direction now. So we have to capitalize on it now while we are young. We have a show coming up soon that Danny promised us. From now on, we are going to do whatever it takes to blow the main act off the stage. I don't care, Marc, if you have to drum naked. I know if we had more money, I would let David smash up my guitars on stage, but we don't, so let's be realistic. We start from the bottom and work our way to the top. Our CD and merchandise sales will increase."

"Do we know yet who we are opening up for?" I asked.

Sebastian answered, "So far I think the band is called Cul-de-sac Kids. Which I give them credit because that name is hilarious. They are more of a punk band from what I heard, but who cares? We are not there to kiss their ass because they are on tour. So let's put our heads together and figure out what to do to make our show better than theirs."

The four of us continued drinking beer and discussing ideas for the upcoming show that we had at Dino's. The free-beer scam worked, but we definitely couldn't use it again.

"How about lasers and fog?" Marc asked.

Sebastian followed up with excitement, "OK, now that's what I'm talking about."

"OK, do any of you know anyone who might have those types of machines?" Anthony mentioned.

I was quick to respond, "Hey, I wonder if Dick would let us borrow some stuff for the show. I can go down there tomorrow and ask him."

Sebastian said, "OK, sounds like a plan. Now let's jump in the other room and hash it out on the instruments." We had a very tight practice and called it a night.

The next day I walked into town to go see Dick. I was about a block away when I heard sirens from an ambulance truck. I looked around because the sirens were getting louder. I couldn't tell which direction they were coming from. Then the sirens stopped, and I said to myself, "Damn, they sound pretty close." I continued walking into town and saw the ambulance parked right in front of Dick's music store. I said to myself again, "Oh shit." I took off running as fast as I could toward the store. I saw a stretcher being wheeled in through the front door. There were a few bystanders talking among themselves and looking through the store window.

As I came up to the front of the store, I said to one of the bystanders, "What happened? Is Dick OK?"

"No, from what I heard, the owner had a heart attack."

I put both my hands on top of my head and said with sadness, "Oh no, this can't be happening."

Then the bystander said, "I don't know what's going to happen to the music equipment. Poor guy, he doesn't have any family after the loss of his son."

I tried to go inside, but a police officer was standing there and said to me, "Hold on, buddy, no one's allowed in there."

"I work for him, and he's like family to me. Please, Officer, I have to go inside."

The officer paused for a second, "OK, since you work here, you can go in."

I walked through the front door and saw a man leaning over Dick's body wearing gloves and a jacket that said coroner on the back. He was lying next to the counter. There were two EMT workers standing nearby with the stretcher. I told everyone in the room who I was and why I was here.

The coroner stood up and said, "Yeah, he is dead. Looks to be the cause of a heart attack." He looked over at the EMTs and said, "OK, gentlemen, you can get him out of here."

I was in total shock and didn't know how to react. As the EMTs were loading his body on to the stretcher, I said, "Hey, before you wheel him out, I would like to say a word if I may."

They replied, "Yeah, sure, go ahead." I had tears filling my eyes as I reached out and grabbed his hand. His hands were cold as ice. His body was stiff as a board. A teardrop landed on his shirt as I said quietly to him, "Dick, I am so sorry that this happened. You were a good friend to me, and I couldn't be more thankful for everything you've done for me. I wish I would have known you a lot longer than we did. I hope you find peace in heaven with your son. Take care, buddy, I will miss you."

I stepped back, and they covered him with a white sheet and wheeled him away. The officer stepped inside the door and said to me, "Sir, I am going to need to leave soon."

I replied, "OK, but what are they going to do now that he is gone?"

He answered, "From what I know, most of the gear will go back to the manufacturers. The rest of it will be given to charity."

Once I heard him say that, I snuck back behind the shop and grabbed the guitar that Dick made for his son. In the eyes of everyone, I was stealing it, but to me, I wasn't. I lied to everyone including the cop saying the guitar was mine, and Dick was working on it. They all bought the story, but I didn't want it to end up in the hands of someone who would tear it up or sell it. I didn't feel bad for what I did. I was going to take extreme care of it, and I knew in my heart that this is what Dick would want. I took the guitar and headed home in tears. What started out as a friend wanting to borrow equipment quickly turned into a nightmare. Dick Newman will always be remembered, and may he rest in peace.

CHAPTER **20**

Carpe Diem Baby

On August 30th, April and I were about to become parents. I managed to make it through the rest of the pregnancy without her trying to kill me. She was nine months and about to pop. Her feet were swollen, and her boobs were enormous. She had a very funny wobble when she walked, and she peed every ten minutes. I couldn't imagine what that felt like having a baby sitting on your bladder all day. I never thought that a woman's belly could get that big, but I was wrong. The day started out pretty normal except for the contractions she was having. We knew that her water could break at any time. I stayed close to her knowing I would be driving her to the hospital.

Around 5:00 PM, we were at the store picking up some last-minute stuff for the baby. We were in the baby section when it all went down. "Oh no!"

I was quick to respond, "What's wrong?"

"Oh god, I think my water just broke. Quick, get me to the hospital now!"

I tried not to panic, but I had to think fast. I yelled in the store, "Help! Can somebody help us please!"

A little stock boy came running around the corner and said, "What's wrong? Is everything OK?"

April screamed, "No, damn it, I am about to have my baby!"

The stock boy about passed out from hearing those words. I said to him, "Buddy, I need you to help her to the exit, I am going to get the car!"

I took off running as fast as I could through the store. I could hear her yelling in the distance, "Hurry, damn it, or I am going to have this baby right here!"

I dropped the keys a couple times trying to open the door. Once I got in, I fired that baby up and drove right up to the entrance. I got back out and headed into the store. I tried not to laugh because all I saw was the innocent little stock boy trying to help April to the front. As he was doing this, April was yelling and smacking him. "Don't touch me, I am trying to move as fast as I can!"

I had grabbed a wheelchair from the front of the store and put her in that. Once I managed to get her into the car, I took off like a bat out of hell. She was in the back seat screaming, "David, hurry, I don't know how much longer I can hold it!"

I yelled back, "Hold on, baby, I am almost there! Just keep taking deep breaths."

The way she was screaming and acting you would have thought that she had a demon in her. I decided to crank up the radio to help keep me focused on the road and to drown out the screams. I had to quit looking into the back seat so I didn't wreck. Go figure, as soon as I turned the radio up, all I heard was the opening piano riff to "Evil Woman" by Electric Light Orchestra. April continued to scream and yell, "Oh, son of a bitch, it hurts! I am going to kill you, David, for putting this thing in me!"

Tires were squealing as I ran stoplights and cut people off until I arrived at the hospital. I pulled up to the emergency entrance and ran inside to get a doctor. I was panting and breathing heavily as I tried to speak to the nurse at the desk. "Help, my girlfriend is about to have her baby!"

The nurse quickly ran around the counter and grabbed a wheelchair. We both headed out the door and got April into the chair, and the nurse rushed her inside. I followed behind as the nurse escorted her through these double doors into the back.

The nurse yelled, "I need Dr. Neil ASAP! She's about to have her baby!"

Another nurse responded, "OK, I will go get him!"

Nurses were scrambling to get everything ready. Once they got her into a room, they laid her on her back. The nurse said, "OK, ma'am, I need you to keep breathing and try to stay calm."

April yelled back, "I'm not going to fucking calm down! I want this thing out of me!" She threw her head back into the pillow and moaned louder.

The nurse looked at me and said, "Sir, please I need you to hold her hand and talk to her. Help her take her mind off what's going on."

I held April's hand, and it felt like it was being crushed by a bulldozer. I put my other hand on her forearm and leaned down next to the bed and said, "Baby, the doctor is coming, and it won't be long, just hang in there." The nurse then stuck an IV in her arm. Everything was going so fast it didn't seem real.

Dr. Neil came into the room wearing his scrubs and face mask. "OK, ladies, what do we got?"

A nurse said out loud, "Patient's name is April Monroe, and she is ten centimeters dilated and ready to give birth."

"OK, let's get started. Hi, April, I need you to put your feet into these stirrups." He put on his gloves and leaned down by her vagina. I stayed up by April's head because I didn't want to see that.

So I didn't look in that direction. The thought of a woman's vagina walls getting stretched that far was enough for me. The doctor put his hands into position and said, "OK, April, on the count of three, I need you to push. One, two, three, push! OK and again, one, two, three, push!"

April was trying her best, and her face was beet red. I couldn't feel my hand anymore. After fifteen minutes of agonizing labor, I heard the screams of a newborn. The doctor stood up with our child and said, "Congratulations, you two, it's a girl."

I had tears in my eyes after seeing my baby girl brought into this world.

Dr. Neil then said, "Sir, would you like to cut the umbilical cord?"

The nurse handed me a pair of scissors, and I went over and cut the cord. A nurse then took her for a second to clean off the blood. Once she was cleaned up, she handed her to her mother. April was so exhausted from the birth, she was about to pass out. She held her baby close to her heart and whispered to me, "She is so gorgeous, isn't she?"

"Most gorgeous baby in the world," I replied.

"I want to name her Emma," April said.

I whispered, "I love it, hello, baby Emma. You were the one causing all the trouble, weren't you?" Her hands and feet were so little as she looked at us with those pretty blue eyes. She had fuzzy brown hair just like me, except mine was longer. I was a father now, and after seeing baby Emma born into this world, it did something to me. I was going to be the most supportive father I can be and give her the life that I wish I had.

CHAPTER 21

Jump in the Fire

A few months went by, and everything was going great. If I wasn't with the guys, I was at home with Emma. Holding her and loving her every minute I was with her. She was a huge part of my life now, and I wouldn't change it for the world. I didn't think being a father and pursuing a rock 'n' roll dream would be that difficult, but things started to get crazy. We took the stage and destroyed the Cul-de-sac Kids. We put on one hell of a show that the main act got booed off-stage. Word of mouth started spreading about us. People started to tune in when they heard the name Amerex. We were getting booked every weekend in all kinds of different clubs and bars. We followed Sebastian's strategy, and it was working very well.

My relationship at home with April was getting stronger because I was starting to bring some money into the house. On January 20, 2001, Waylon came through for us, and we got the most exciting news at practice. The phone rang, and Sebastian answered it, "Hello, this is Sebastian Rose with Amerex. Can I help you?" He put his hand over the mouth speaker and whispered loudly to us, "Holy shit, this guy says he is with Unique Records!"

We all put our instruments down and ran over to him. Sebastian put the call on speaker phone so we all could hear.

The guy said, "My name is Chad McCormick, and I am the executive here at Unique Records. I have been hearing a lot about you guys, and I finally got a chance to listen to your demo. I'm sure you guys are familiar with a guy named Waylon Boise."

Sebastian replied, "Yes, he was the one that recorded the demo."

"Yeah, and so I would like for you boys to come to my office here in Columbus on January 24 at 11:00 AM. I have a very busy schedule, so I wouldn't be late if I were you."

"We will be there at ten forty-five just to be safe," Sebastian hollered.

"OK, see you then, gentlemen." He hung up the phone, and we jumped around acting like a bunch of high school girls. This was the break we were looking for ever since we started this band.

I went home that night and immediately grabbed Emma and started dancing and singing to her. April was sitting on the couch looking at me like I was insane. She said, "Hi, baby, looks like you're in a good mood."

I was holding Emma and said, "Yes, today was a great day, and do you want to know why?"

"Yes, of course, I do."

I yelled, "We have a meeting in Columbus with an executive from Unique Records. We hope that this is the break we have been looking for!"

April stood up and gave me a hug saying, "Congratulations, baby, that's great to hear. So when is your meeting?"

"Here in a couple days. If this goes well, we will have a record deal and all kinds of good stuff coming our way. More money will start coming in, and maybe you could quit your job."

April said, "Oh, that would be nice, but I won't hold my breath on it. You guys need to be smart about this and make sure you're not going to get screwed in the end."

"Trust me, baby, we got this," I said.

April then grabbed my head and kissed me on the lips and said that she loved me.

When the day came, we all jumped into the van and headed up to Columbus. It was about an hour-and-a-half drive. The four of us were on a mission to sell ourselves. We had to be professional and not act stupid because these people were all about business. We arrived at this office building that was three stories high. Once we parked, Sebastian said to us, "Guys, I am very proud of all of you. We have worked very hard, and no matter what happens in this meeting, just know we aren't slowing down."

Anthony said, "You're damn right, brother, and I love you, guys. I mean it, I am very thankful for being a part of this."

"Yeah, me too, now let's go in there and do it," Marc added.

I thought this was a perfect time to mess with them so I said, "Hey, guys, this might not be the time, but I don't know if I can do this anymore."

They all three gave me the look of death as I burst out laughing and said, "I'm just fucking with you, guys!" Sebastian leans over and punches me in the shoulder and yells, "Oh, you asshole, don't scare me like that! Now get out of the van and let's go."

As we walked through the front door, there was an elevator and a directory hanging up on the wall. There were all kinds of other businesses, and so we looked for Unique Records. It was located on the third floor in suite 320. We went up and walked into suite 320. There was a receptionist sitting at a desk. She said, "Can I help you, gentlemen?"

"Yes, we have an eleven o'clock meeting with Chad McCormick," Sebastian answered.

"OK, who are you with?"

"Amerex."

"OK, just one minute please." She reached down and picked up the phone. Then she said, "Chad, I have four gentlemen out here that go by the name Amerex." There was a pause for a second, and then she followed up with, "OK, thanks, I will send them back. OK, gentlemen, please follow me."

We followed the lady around the corner and down a hall. She said to us as we approached an office door, "Here you go, gentlemen, Mr. McCormick will see you now." We walked into this small conference room, and Mr. McCormick was sitting at the far end of the table wearing a suit and tie. He stood up and said, "You boys must be Amerex. Been hearing a lot about you, please take a seat anywhere you like. There is coffee if you guys want any."

I sat next to Sebastian while Anthony and Marc sat across from us. This was a nice room, carpeted floors with a drop ceiling. The big table was made out of oak, and the chairs were leather. We introduced ourselves one by one. Sebastian said, "Nice to meet you, Chad, my name is Sebastian Rose, and I am the front man."

"I am Marc Allenhart, and I play the drums."

"I'm Anthony Martini, and I'm the bassist."

Then I said, "My name is David Taylor, and I am the lead guitar player. Thanks for having us."

Chad sat back into his chair and said, "So I bet you boys are wondering why you are here. Your buddy Waylon talked us into listening to your demo. I am going to be honest. I ignored his request for quite some time until I kept hearing your name pop up at venues nearby. So I listened to it, and I was impressed with the sound you boys are creating. Here at Unique Records, we are very picky about the bands we work with, but I know there is a good market out there with your sound. I want to know if you boys have more tunes, and if so, I would like to contract you boys in. Unique Records will record your first album and follow it up with tour dates. I have the contract ready for you boys to sign. So what do you say, boys, shall we proceed?"

The four of us huddled close and whispered among ourselves. Marc said, "Hell, yeah, let's do this. We could become rock stars overnight."

Anthony didn't think twice he was in.

I said, "Guys, shouldn't we have someone like a lawyer look at this before we sign it?"

Sebastian kinda agreed with me and said to Chad, "We want to take this contract and have someone look at it."

Chad's facial expression didn't look pleased. He followed up with, "Gentlemen, you either sign now, or the deal is off, it's up to you."

Now we had no other choice. Sebastian said to us, "This may be our only opportunity, guys. What do we got to lose?" Sebastian looked back over at Chad and said, "Sounds like you got yourself a deal."

Chad pulled out the contract, and we all four signed it. Once the signing was done, he said, "Congratulations, boys. First things first, I will have some recording dates lined up, and the guy who will be managing is named Rocky Owens. He will make sure things get done. Glad to have you be a part of Unique Records."

When I got back home, I ran through the house with my guitar around my neck. I was jamming along with the radio cranked up. I was superstoked, and when April got home with Emma, I told her the news. I yelled as she came through the door, "Baby, we did it! We got our first record deal!"

She smiled and replied, "Oh, that's great, hun, I am so proud of you! Lean over here, and tell your daughter."

I leaned over her baby seat to kiss her, and I said, "Emma, Daddy is one step closer to his dream, and I know you and Mommy are going to be proud of me."

April said, "Let me go lay her down for a little bit, and I want some more details about what's going on." She went and laid Emma down, and then we both sat down on the couch facing each other, and something changed in her. "So what's all going to happen now that you're signed?"

"All that I know as of now is that we have recording dates coming up fast, and we have this manager named Rocky Owens who will be managing us and our tour."

She said immediately, "Wait, what! A tour, what kind of tour are we talking about here?"

"After we record the album, we have to tour for a while. That's how we are going to make money. I don't know all the details on the tour yet until we're done recording."

The look on April's face wasn't pleasant, and she said with anger, "You can't leave me and Emma for that long. You're a father now, and I need you here at home with us."

I started getting a little testy. "Babe, listen to me, this is going to be great. Once we get through the first couple tours, I know that I will be able to give you and Emma a better life."

The arguing began as she said, "A better life, how is that? You will never be home, and who knows what you will do on the road with those guys? I will not tolerate girls wanting to sleep with you every night. I guarantee that the first opportunity you get to sleep with a girl, you will, and I would never know!"

I yelled, "I can't fucking believe you right now, you are acting insane! You were very supportive the other day, and now that I tell you this, it's all changed! I'm not in this business to bang any girl I want."

She yelled back, "Yeah, well, that changed when you became a father! I need help with Emma, if I have to do this alone, then I won't need you in my life."

I started shaking real bad. I would never hit a girl, but in my mind, I wanted to bust her in her mouth. I yelled some more, "I have been through a lot of shit in my life, and I finally have a chance to make my dreams come true! Out of all people, I thought you would understand!"

She said, "I am happy for you, but I won't let you come in and out of her life with you touring like this! I won't! It will confuse her."

I continued, "The tour hasn't even happened yet! She's just a baby. She's not even old enough to know what's going on. I can see why you would be a little upset, but damn, April, you are starting to show your true colors!"

She fired back, "You're mad because you know I am right!"

Again, I continued to yell, "So what! You going to give me an ultimatum, is that it?"

She started calming down and said in a lower tone, "No, I am not giving you an ultimatum, David. I would never do that, I am just scared for what the future might have in store for us. Once Emma was born, I changed. It's not about us anymore, it's about her. I don't think now is the perfect time for you to be leaving."

"I agree the timing is not the best, but look at me please. You got to believe in me, and I know in my heart that this band will be on top real soon. You said it yourself when we first met, and I really hope you meant it. Anyway I am tired of arguing, and Emma will be up soon."

We both were running out of steam by this point. I loved her, but I was sticking to my guns this time. I signed a contract and couldn't back out now. I was going to continue rolling the dice and see what happens.

CHAPTER 22

Where The Wild Things Are

It was time for Amerex to professionally record our first album. We had to drive to Grove City to meet Rocky at this place called Sonic Lounge Studios. When we arrived, the place looked like a small brick house. We drove past the place a couple times because it blended in with its surroundings. We finally figured it out when we saw a short chubby guy with a really bad comb-over standing in this parking lot.

"I think that is the manager, so pull in there and ask him," Marc said.

We met our manager Rocky Owens for the first time. This guy definitely reminded us of Danny DeVito. He introduced himself as we stepped out of the van. "Hello, fellows, I am Rocky, and I will be your manager/tour manager. We are glad to have you be a part of Unique Records. Chad has been bragging you guys up, and so I will be taking care of everything from here on out. All you boys have to do is focus on your music. First things first, we will be here for a couple weeks recording, and then we have a full tour schedule lined up for you. So come on in guys and check out the studio and meet the producer."

We walked up these concrete steps and headed in through the back door. The first thing we saw was the break room. It had a small sink and fridge along with a big screen and video game console. There was a small glass table and big couch to relax on.

Anthony was like, "All right, video games, that will come in handy."

Then Rocky took us down the hallway that had records hanging all down it. We came up on a double glass door that led to this big room. He said, "Gentlemen, this is where we will be recording the drums."

Marc was about to nut in his pants because he thought it was so nice. There was a bunch of superexpensive microphones hooked up to these mic stands. The floor was hardwood with a big piece of carpet on top. The walls had sound-damping foam all around it. Attached to the big room were two smaller rooms with amplifiers hooked up inside. A single glass door and a double door separated these rooms. The drum room also had a massive double window looking into the master control room. Through the glass, we could see a long blond-hair dude who looked to be working on something. He looked up at us through the glass and waved us to come into the other room. Rocky said, "OK, guys, let's go meet Joe Collins, he will be producing your album."

We had to go back out the room and down the hallway to get to the control room. Inside this room, we were blown away at the size of the mixing board. We had never seen so many buttons and dial knobs. The room had two big TVs above the mixing board. Another couch was along the opposite side of the wall. There was another single glass door that led to the vocal booth. He had a computer stand with a Macintosh computer. The program he had running on the screen said Pro Tools. The four of us were just dazed at all this nice equipment. Joe turned around to introduce himself. "Hey, guys, my name is Joe Collins, and I will be your lead engineer and producer and welcome to my studio. I see that Rocky already gave you a small tour, and I am glad that we will be working together."

Sebastian and Joe shook hands. "Nice to meet you, Joe, I am Sebastian the vocalist, and this is my drummer Marc Allenhart and bassist Anthony Martini. This gentleman to the left of me is David Taylor, our guitar player. By the way, this place is amazing."

"Glad to meet you, guys, and thank you. I put a lot of money into it, and it's been paying off over the years."

"That mixing board looks like something from the future. What is that?" Marc asked.

Joe explained, "This right here is where the magic happens. This is a 48-channel Amek 9098i design by Mr. Rupert Neve. It was the most important landmark in the history of analogue console development, and here it is. Featuring an extended audio bandwidth of 200 kHz (-3dB), the 9098i maintains a sense of transparency that is absent from inferior bandwidth limited systems. This has an incredible dynamic range, and the remarkable phase linearity provides accurate imaging across the entire bandwidth. With virtual class A operation throughout, it provides a sense of realism other consoles simply cannot produce. This is achieved by reducing distortion to a barely measurable level. There were only thirteen of these manufactured worldwide, and I purchased mine out of the Olympic Studios in London. Some very well-known artists have recorded on this including Eric Clapton, the Spice Girls, and David Gilmour of Pink Floyd."

I interrupted and said, "That is badass, Joe, and how long have you been doing this?"

"I have been doing this for over twenty-five years. I have worked with some of the greatest artists ever known. However, gentlemen, I don't want to sound rude, but I could sit here all day and tell you everything about me, but we are on a production schedule, so it's time for us to get to work. We only have three weeks to record ten tracks and have them mastered."

We all had so many questions for him and yet so little time. Joe was in charge, and it was time to go. He said, "Marc, I need you to go ahead and load your drums in that room and start setting up. The rest of you can bring your instruments in and get them tuned up and ready to go."

We went to the trailer and started unpacking all the gear. Marc's drums were going to take a minute because of all the microphones Joe had to set up. I was going to be using Dick's guitar and Sebastian's Les Paul for tracking all the guitar parts. Marc had this headset on, so Joe could communicate to him on what to do. He said to us, "The rest of you guys, hang tight for a bit, until I get these drums ready."

It took almost three hours to get the drums set up and dialed in. Joe went through every single drum piece to make sure it was equalized. Joe was very picky about the drum sound, and he wasn't a guy who wouldn't proceed unless he had it dialed in just right. It was so cool seeing all the microphones hooked up to Marc's kit. I could tell Marc felt like a rock star as I watched him drum check from the control room. The next thing we did was go out into the main room with Marc. Joe hooked up our instruments and said, "Right now, guys, we are just tracking scratch tracks of all the tunes, so we can get a feel for what the tempo of the songs should be. After that, we will just focus on Marc for a few days. Once he is done, then we will move to all the bass tracks, then guitar, and vocals are last." That moment I knew there was going to be a lot of downtime in between each person. That explains the video-game system in the other room.

Rocky had a hotel lined up for us for the entire time we were here. He also had supplied all our meals along with it. To me it felt like prison again but a very nice prison with benefits. After each ten-hour day in the studio, I would call home from the hotel room to check on April. She wasn't liking it too much, but what girl wouldn't at first? It was going to take some time getting used to it. We were four days in when tensions started rising between Marc and Sebastian.

Joe was almost done with recording the drums, and Marc was taking forever on this complicated drum fill. For some reason, he was just struggling with some parts, and Sebastian would say shit to him.

Sebastian spoke through the talk-back mic from the control room to Marc, "Marc, hurry the hell up, or I will come in there and do it for you."

We could hear him yell back through the instrument mics. He yelled, "Fuck you, man, I have been in here for thirty hours, and I'm fucking worn-out, so give me a break. Just wait until you get to sing your parts, asshole!" Sebastian didn't like what he had to say, so he walked around to the room to confront Marc.

Joe sat at the console and said to me, "Give them a second, and let them work it out. You boys are in the early stages of studio fever, and it's going to get a hell of a lot worse. I see this all the time with different bands." Joe left the microphones on so we could hear them. They started arguing over the dumbest shit, and they weren't slowing down, so Rocky eventually had to step in and break it up. Rocky said, "Marc, take five and go outside for a little bit. Sebastian, please go relax in the other room with Joe or do something."

It only took about ten minutes for everything to calm down.

When Marc came into the control room, Joe decided to tell us a funny, disgusting story to help ease the stress and make us laugh. We were all sitting on the couch, and as he went on to explain, he said, "I did this session with a band once, and they were in here for five weeks recording. The last day, the manager decided to hire a stripper. So this girl comes over, and she's kinda nasty."

We all started giggling as he continued, "Like she wasn't even cute enough to be a drunk fuck. So she starts doing her thing and whips out the bag of toys and starts shoving shit up in her. Then she breaks out the lollipop and sticks it in her puss and then sticks it in this dude's mouth, and he fucking let her do it! And then later on, like ten minutes later, she pulls out this dildo and puts him on the ground. She shoves the back end on it in his mouth and gets on it and starts going on this thing. I'm thinking how in the hell is he not vomiting right now."

The four of us started to burst out laughing at this point. Joe went on, "This girl, I wouldn't want anywhere near my face or anything that was in her body inside my mouth. I said to the guy, 'are you on crack or something?' I guess he was one of their techs or something." Joe's story was quite detailed, but it helped loosen up the mood in the room, and everything started getting back to normal. Marc went back into the drum room and nailed out the rest of his tracks. Up next was the bass tracking. It didn't take long to get the bass set up and dialed in. Joe was a bass player himself so he and Anthony got along real well. The most annoying thing to Anthony was hearing that click track. This was a guide to keeping everyone at the right tempo. It only took fifteen hours to get all the bass tracks finished. The first week had come to an end, and we had all the drums and bass tracked. We were off to a good start.

When it was my turn, I was the most concerned because I was laying down all the rhythm parts and guitar solos. I had some issues playing live with trying to play the same guitar solo over and over. The first song I decided to record was a song called "Into the Night." This was the most difficult track on the album for soloing, and so I thought I should knock it out first. I said to Joe, "Hey, let's record this track first because of the solo."

He said to me, "David, we are not going to worry about the solos just yet. We are going to track all the rhythm parts, and then we will do the leads last." He was the boss, and so we tracked all the rhythm parts first. We used a couple different types of amps to get the sound he was looking for. Joe had a very good ear; he would know exactly when the guitar was out of tune. I guess after doing this for twenty-five years, you would have a magic ear too. Plus how embarrassing and unprofessional it would be if someone else noticed that your instrument was out of tune on your album. Recording for me was very stressful and took me forty hours to track everything. When I was done, I felt like my brain had overheated, but I managed to get through it, and I was proud of my work, and so were the guys. You could tell Joe was getting worn-out. He started coming into the studio in the morning, and his eyes would be bloodshot. He loved his job, and that's what kept him going.

Sebastian had waited the longest, and now it was time for him to record. He had to be careful because if he blew his voice out, we would be screwed. So Rocky recommended some helpful tips for him to keep his voice in shape. Every morning he was doing thirty-minute exercises and drinking green tea and honey. The honey acted like a lubricant, like a fresh new oil change for a car. Sebastian was smart with his voice. He knew that it was his instrument and his moneymaker, so he would not drink certain types of liquids during this process. The voice can only take so many hours of recording, and Sebastian had to take frequent breaks. Joe would track one verse at a time and then the choruses. After tracking that, the final step would be adding layers and harmonies. Nothing made the songs better than adding harmonies. Sebastian laid most of his harmonies because he was the better singer. However, during live shows, Anthony and I would sing the harmonies. After two and a half weeks of recording, all tracks were finished. The only steps left were for mixing and mastering. The four of us were walking, talking zombies. We didn't do much physical work, but mentally we were drained.

Rocky threw us a party on the last day in the studio to celebrate. Thank God he didn't hire any strippers because after what Joe told us, I have a different look at strippers. Rocky bought us some expensive-ass champagne. He popped the bottle and poured us all a drink. He raised his glass and said, "Gentlemen, congrats on your first album. I want to let you know that we only have a couple of weeks of downtime, and then the six-month tour begins. So here is to Amerex's first album called *Turn Up the Heat!*" All of us raised our glasses and toasted to the album. When I was taking a drink, I got a little nervous because Rocky just said we would be doing a six-month tour. I knew that April was going to have a shit fit when she heard this.

CHAPTER 23

Attitude

It was a long, stressful few weeks of recording, but it was time for us to head home. I was missing Emma more than ever. No matter how bad of a day I was having, her smile and laughter would make it all better. I wouldn't think about anything but her when I was with her, and so I had to take this time to soak up as much as I could before I leave again. Emma was at the early stages of trying to walk. It was the cutest thing watching her try to walk. She had the crawling thing down pat, and boy, let me tell you if you weren't watching her close, she would be all over the place. I was lucky enough to catch her first word. I was playing with her in the living room one evening when I heard her say, "Dada."

April came running into the room and said, "Oh, did I just hear her say a word?"

I was lying on the carpet and replied with excitement, "I think she just said *dada*, but I wasn't sure."

April picked Emma up and held her close to her face and said, "Can you say *mama*? Come on, gorgeous, I know you can do it. Say *mama*."

Emma just stared at her for a second, and then she said it again, "Dada."

My face lit up with joy as I got up from the floor. I said, "I knew it, she said dada." I squeezed her cheeks and gave her a big kiss on the forehead.

April was very distant with me ever since I got back. It's almost like I was not even there sometimes. Later that night, I had to sit her down and break the news to her. Emma went to bed around 8:00 PM, and I was sitting at the kitchen table. I called for April, "Hey, darling, could I have a word with you?"

Took a few seconds for her to reply as she was in the other room. "Yeah, what do you want, David?"

I replied without trying to wake Emma up, "I just want to have a talk please, I miss you."

"Give me a second, and I will be right there." She came into the kitchen and sat at the table across from me. She had this look of fatigue as she said, "What do you want to talk about, David?"

"First off, I just want to say that I love you and miss you and Emma. Ever since I got back, you have been distant from me. I do have some things I would like to talk to you about if you promise not to throw a temper tantrum."

She put both elbows on the table with one hand on her face. She said, "Oh, good, because I have some things that I would like to talk about too."

"OK, well, how about you go first, and I won't interrupt."

She went on to explain, "I've been doing a lot of thinking lately especially since you've been gone. I have been going back and forth in my head for the past couple weeks, and I am not sure if I can do this whole band thing anymore. I was so stressed out while taking care of Emma all by myself while you were recording. I thought you were going through a phase and maybe break out of it after once she was born, but I was wrong. I need you here more often, and if you can't do it, then I don't need you. I won't tolerate you out doing what you love and partying while I stay home and take care of a baby. I am sorry, but I have to put my foot down on this."

I was in total shock. I was starting to feel heartbroken. The woman I loved pretty much said she was done with me. I followed up with, "How could you say that after everything we've been through? Plus you knew that music was my life before all this. The band just got signed to a record deal, and we just wrapped up with a very badass album, and I come home to this. Things are going strong, and now you're dumping this shit on me."

"Things are going good for you, David, not our relationship. Sometimes I think all you care about is that damn band," she said.

I raised my voice a little. "No, that is not true, I love you and Emma just as much as I love those guys. That really hurts my feelings for you to say that. I went up to Columbus and busted my ass, and I called you almost every other night, so don't say that I don't care."

"You don't get it, that band may not be around forever. I know that me and Emma are your family, and we will always be around."

I was getting angry, and you could see it in my face.

I replied, "Yeah, well, how do I know that you will be around forever? You could leave me anytime you want, and it sounds like you are."

She said, "We just had a beautiful baby girl, and nothing in this world would make me more happy than her father being around to see her grow up. Shortly after she was born, you go record for three weeks, and now you have a tour coming up. I want to know how long is that tour going to be? I swear to God, if it's longer than a couple months, I am going to flip shit."

I paused for a sec and put my head down. I raised my head back up and said, "Rocky told us that the tour was around six months, and I leave in a week."

145

April put both hands over her eyes and started crying. She mumbled as she was crying, "You asshole, when were you going to tell me this? What am I going to do now?"

I was torn inside watching her break down and cry like that. I know she loves me and wants me to be here. I had to follow my heart, and my heart wanted me to go on tour. After she started calming down, she took her hands off her face and reached for a tissue. She blew her nose and said to me, "I tell you what, I love you with all my heart, but if you go on tour, I don't know if I will be here when you get back."

The only response I could come up with was, "So what about our military men and women who leave their families to go fight? It's OK for them to be gone that long?"

April replied with frustration, "That is totally different. They are fighting for our country."

I started laughing like an asshole. I said, "Wow, sounds like you really don't like my band. Thank you, babe, for all the support which turned out to be one big lie." I was being a sarcastic prick by now.

April said one last time to me, "I want you out of this house for good. You just told me your heart was with your band, and so go be with them. This relationship is over, David, and I will be getting full custody of Emma. I will not allow her father to come in and out of her life."

I lost control of my anger and stood up from the table and yelled, "Fuck you, bitch! How could you be like this! One day you're going to regret leaving my ass when my band is on top of the world! Then I will watch you struggle, and I will be the one laughing!" I could hear Emma starting to cry in the distance. Those cries were enough to make me stop yelling and try to run to her aid.

As I started running, April yelled, "Don't you touch her, asshole! You have ten seconds to get out of this house, or I am calling the cops!" I knew she was going to call the law, so I quickly grabbed my stuff and headed out the door. Once I was heading out the door, I turned to her and said, "When I get back from the tour, I will see your ass in court, bitch."

CHAPTER 24

The Struggle Within

Touring day had arrived, and the four of us were superstoked. I had stayed at Sebastian's until it was time. We had to take all the gear back up to Columbus to meet with Rocky. We were parked right out back when Rocky pulled up in this badass silver 1955 Vista liner tour bus. To many people, this was a piece of shit, but we had to work our way up the chain. I loved it, and I looked at the guys and said, "This can't be for us!"

"Oh, boys, I think it is!" Sebastian hollered.

The door opened, and Rocky stepped out and said, "Gentlemen, sorry to keep you waiting, but are you ready to tour?"

We all yelled, "Hell, yeah!"

"All right then, grab your shit, and let's roll. We got to be in Pittsburgh by five," he announced.

We loaded all our gear into the undercarriage. There was enough room under there to stuff twenty dead bodies. As I headed into the bus, I saw an old man sitting behind the wheel with a Lynyrd Skynyrd bandana and a cigar in his mouth. He had a white beard and tattoos and also had a blue-jean jacket vest on. He said, "Hey, fellows, my name is Bob Fuller, and I will be your driver. I only have a few rules on this bus, and they are clean up your stains and no pissing in the beds. Oh, and if you bring any girls on board, I get a free ass shot with my camera."

He had a very deep sense of humor, and his smoker's voice made it even funnier.

"I think we can manage that, and I definitely like this bus, Bob," Sebastian commented.

"Yeah, her same is Sally, and she purrs like a kitten," Bob said.

Once we got familiar with Bob, we looked around the inside of the bus. There was a couch along one side with a small table with four seats and a tiny kitchen with a counter and sink. In the very back, there were four bunk beds stacked two on each side. I felt like a touring rock star, and we haven't even began. Then, Bob yelled, "All right, boys, it's time to hit the road! Next stop is Pittsburgh, Pennsylvania." Bob cranked up the CD, and "Spirit of the Radio" by Rush started playing. I love the opening of that song. Rocky taped the tour schedule to the mini fridge that was under the counter. The cities we were going to were Pittsburgh, Charlotte, Jacksonville, Nashville, Chicago, and the list went on and on.

When we arrived in Pittsburgh, we went through this long tunnel that went through a mountain. At the end of the tunnel, you could see light, and then we saw the beautiful city of Pittsburgh. At that moment, I felt this was my destiny. Coming into a big city as a bunch of strangers and leaving like rock stars. The four of us set out to become the next biggest rock band of all time. We were opening for another band that Unique Records had signed with for a long time. They had a well-established fan base, and they could put on one hell of a show.

As much fun and excitement as this may sound, it wasn't that easy of a job. Loading gear in and out was stressful depending on the venues. We didn't have the luxury like the other band did of having our own sound guy and full road crew, so we had to deal with what the venues offered us. We had to stick to a very strict set time and not go over it. If we went over our time, they would kill the sound, and you had no other choice but to step off. So we had to work extra hard as a band to put on a great show, so people would buy our album and merchandise. That first impression would make or break us in these cities. Once the shows were over, we were off to the next city, then off to the next. There was absolutely no slowing down, and I wasn't getting enough sleep on the bus.

Running around on stage every night with three sweaty men was taking a toll on me. The guys would party after every show. They love to drink, but I quickly found out that wasn't the only thing they liked to do. I knew something wasn't right when I would go to bed, and I would hear them in the front of the bus. I went up there one late night and saw all three of them sitting around the little table snorting something.

I said with fatigue, "What the hell are you guys doing?"

"Oh, hey, David, just having a little fun," Marc mentioned.

"Yeah, dude, come join us, and do some blow, you deserve it." Anthony said after ripping a line.

Sebastian stood up and walked over and put his arm around me and said, "David, I want you to know that this helps up get through some of the shows. I know you have been very tired lately, but you could use a little for the show coming up."

In my mind, drugs are what got me sentenced to prison, and since I wasn't dealing, I caved into peer pressure. I said, "Yeah, what the hell, we came this far, I guess, it wouldn't hurt to do a little."

The three of them yelled, "Hell, yeah, that's our boy!"

Bob turned around from the driver's seat and said, "How the hell do you boys think I can drive all day and night?" Bob started laughing and carrying on. Marc fixed me up a line and handed me a rolled-up dollar bill. I leaned over and snorted a massive line of coke.

My heart rate started racing immediately, and I had energy, lots of energy.

Sebastian says to me, "How do you feel now, David?"

I paused for a second and looked at the three of them and yelled, "I feel alive! I feel like I could run ten miles and not stop!" We all burst out laughing and continued to do some more. Cocaine was a hell of a drug, and it helped me stay awake for sure. I liked it so much I would spend half my money on it. It became a routine thing right before shows. We would gather around the table in the bus and rip a few lines before we would take the stage. When I was on coke, I wouldn't think about anything but music. Everything else didn't matter in my life. I was starting to revert back to my old bad habits.

After a show in Kansas, I was high on coke and met a couple groupies. They approached me at our merch table. They both had long blond hair and green eyes. Both were wearing sexy leather that was skin tight. Sebastian was standing next to me when he elbowed me and whispered, "Look what's coming our way, David."

They approached us, and one said, "Hi, boys, that was an amazing show tonight. My friend and I wanted to come over and meet you."

Sebastian took the lead on this one and replied, "Nice to meet you, lovely ladies, and glad you enjoyed the show. Would you like to buy a CD, and we will sign it?"

One girl leaned over the table and said in a sexy voice, "We didn't come over here to buy CDs." That was the signal that we knew what they were after. Marc and Anthony happened to be walking by the table at that time. Sebastian said to them, "Hey, guys, you need to watch the table for a little bit. These lovely ladies would like to see the tour bus." Sebastian winked at them, and they weren't stupid. They knew what was about to happen. I reached out and grabbed one by the hand, and so did Sebastian. We took them back to the bus. Bob was passed out on the couch. So we went into the back, and the bus started rocking.

Being high on coke, I was able to keep going and going just like the Energizer Bunny. Sebastian was a sex god; the moaning that was coming out of her mouth was very loud. My girl was freakin', and she liked it hard too, and after a while, we swapped girls and kept going. We established a big rule, and that was if the bus is a-rocking, don't come a-knocking. After we got done banging these girls, we sent them back and headed to the next city. The fucked-up thing was I didn't even think about April the entire time I was gone. It's never a good idea to get in a fight with your woman right before you leave for a while. I could only imagine she was fucking someone else by now. I would think about Emma on some occasions when I wasn't high. I was missing her smiles and giggles. She was growing up without me being there. Every chance I got, I would try to call back home, but April wouldn't answer. I just wanted to hear Emma's voice and tell her I loved her.

Three months into the tour, we got news from Chad that a band had dropped off a bill and we would be filling in the spot. It was a big outdoor festival in Dallas, Texas. There was going to be thirty bands playing and some big upcoming artists including Seether, Three Days Grace, Chevelle, etc. This was probably going to big one of the biggest stops on our tour. It was going to be a great opportunity for us to really make some noise.

When we got to Dallas, it was hot as hell. Temperatures in Dallas could reach up to almost one hundred degrees in the summer. We were going to be opening up on the second stage. We pulled into the back next to some of the most badass tour buses I had ever seen. One of the stage managers for the show gave us our backstage passes and parking permit. We were going to take the stage early, and we didn't have much time to screw around. We had to be ready by 11:00 AM and be on stage by noon. It didn't take long to get the stage set and sound checked. The doors opened at eleven thirty, and there were hundreds of people waiting outside the gates to get in.

Once the gates opened, there were all kinds of vendors and things to do. We figured not a lot of people would come to the front of the stage because we were nobodies, but at least they would hear us. I was backstage with the guys pacing back and forth; I was so nervous. Marc was breathing heavily while stretching his arms and legs. Sebastian was warming up his voice in the bus. Anthony had to take a shit; he was so nervous.

Then it was time for us to take the stage. Sebastian stepped out of the bus with the look of determination. I had my guitar strapped around my neck as I stepped out on to the stage. It was by far the biggest stage I have played on so far. Marc got behind the drum kit while Anthony took his side of the stage. The crowd was bigger than we expected. At least a couple thousand were standing in front waiting to hear what we got. I was about to puke my guts out. I had to stay focused as I strummed the opening chords to our song. Marc and Anthony came in strong, and off we went. Sebastian runs out from behind Marc and grabs the mic putting his fist in the air and yelling, "Dallas, Texas, are you ready? We are Amerex, and we are from Ohio, so let's gooooooo!"

Sebastian had that crowd going ape shit from the first song to the last. Once I got through that first song, my nerves calmed down, and I was having fun. We only had a thirty-minute set time, and we made it worth every minute. Our legacy was growing stronger every show we played, and this one definitely went down as one of the best so far. Rocky came up to us backstage after the show and yelled, "That was kick ass, guys! Now get out there, and sign some autographs because people are waiting."

I congratulated the guys and started to head toward the crowd. I was wiping the sweat off my face with a towel as a couple of police officers approached me out of nowhere and said, "Sir, is your name David Taylor?"

"Yes, sir, that's me, is everything all right?"

The officer said, "Not really, we better talk in private."

I was stunned and in shock thinking what could be wrong. I said, "OK, come with me. We can talk out back by the buses."

Once we got back there, "So what seems to be the problem?" I asked.

The two officers had the look of sadness on their faces. Then one said, "There has been an accident back home involving your daughter Emma. I am afraid to say your daughter Emma has been killed in a terrible car wreck. A drunk driver blew through a stop sign and hit the back passenger side of the car where your daughter was. I got the call about an hour ago from Ohio. I had to come track you down and tell you. I am so sorry, David, to bring you this news. If there is anything I can do, please let me know."

My heart sank into my stomach as I fell back against the bus. I slid down to the ground and started balling my eyes out. I clinched my fist and yelled, "No! No! No! This can't be real. Tell me this isn't happening?"

The cop replied, "I am so sorry, David, I really wish it wasn't real."

I tried to ask the officer about April as I was choking on my tears. "What about April? Is she OK?"

He paused for a second and said, "She has some broken bones but is in stable condition, and that's all I know. If you want, we could take you to the bus stop, so you can catch a ride back home."

I replied with a face full of tears, "OK, just give me a second." I got up and ran back on to the bus to grab my stuff. Rocky saw me and immediately ran over and said, "Whoa, whoa, whoa, what are you doing, David?"

"I have to go home, Rocky, it's an emergency."

He replied in a frantic voice, "What the hell, man, you just can't leave, we still have more shows to do!" He tried to stop me as I was walking out the bus.

I dropped my gear, slammed him up against the bus and yelled, "You don't fucking understand, do you? I have to go home! So go fuck yourself and this tour!" I let go of him and went on my way.

In the background, I could hear Rocky yelling, "Fine, go home! I will make sure that you will never step on a stage ever again!"

I didn't say a word to the guys; I just left the tour and didn't look back.

CHAPTER 25

Suicide & Redemption

Taking a Greyhound bus back to Ohio was one of the most dreadful experiences. Thoughts of Emma were racing through my brain as I sat next to the window. A little girl sat next to me playing with her dolls. She would say to her father, "Daddy, look, I made her hair all pretty just like mine." I couldn't look away from the window as it was too much to take. I could see in the reflection on the glass the bags under my eyes from the loss of sleep. I had a massive headache from all the crying, and my hair was a long greasy mess.

Took a few days, but once I got back to Ohio, I took a cab back to the house. The sky was dark and overcast as I was dropped off at the street corner. There I stood like a ghost staring at the house. I was afraid to go inside. I was hoping this was all a bad dream, and I would wake up soon. I eventually went inside and back to Emma's room. I slowly opened the door and saw April had pictures of her everywhere. Her toys were all over the room, and there on the dresser was the last picture taken of me and Emma. My lips started shaking as I grabbed the picture and pretended I was holding her. I looked over and saw her favorite teddy bear lying in her crib. I reached down and picked up the bear. I held it close to my face and began to cry.

I cried to myself, "Emma, I am so sorry. I wish I would have never left you in the first place. You meant the world to me, and I wish it was me instead of you. You deserved better, and Daddy was just trying to give you a life that I didn't have. I said some horrible things to your mother that I wish I didn't say."

The tears came even harder as I said, "I love you, baby boo, and I want you to know that Daddy is a fuckup. I remember that night you came into this world." I couldn't hold it in and fell to my knees and yelled, "Oh, God, why? Why did you take my baby girl from me!"

I looked to the ceiling and continued crying, "What do you want from me? Was I that bad of a person to deserve all this?" I cried and I cried, and then I went into the kitchen and grabbed a bottle of whiskey I had stored away. I didn't want to feel any more pain, so I sat at the kitchen table and drank and drank. I chugged that bottle in less than five minutes.

The clock on the wall said it was 2:30 AM. I looked over and saw the answering machine flashing one new voicemail. I reached over and hit Play. All I heard next was, "David, it's Sebastian, I figured this was the only way to get my message to you. I am sorry for the loss of your child, I really am. I don't know how else to put this, but we had to replace you. You walking off the tour in Dallas really pissed off the record label. Not only did you walk out on them, but you walked out on us, and so we had to hire this new guy named Cameron. He is a great guitar player, and he will be your replacement. We should have read that deal before we all signed it, but there is nothing we can do now. If we had more control than the label, you know we would have stopped the tour for a few weeks. I hope this doesn't cause any bad blood between us, but Amerex has to keep going on. I hope someday you will get back on your feet. However, I want to thank you for being a part of my life and the band's. I wish you the best of luck, take care, Sebastian."

After hearing that, I grabbed the answering machine and threw it across the kitchen, breaking it into a bunch of pieces. I was thinking if there could be anything else that would go fucking wrong in my life. I was drunk and emotional, two of the worse combinations.

I headed out of the house and went for a walk. I walked and I walked and I walked. Raindrops started falling from the sky. I had the picture of me and Emma in my hand. As I headed toward town, the rain starting coming down harder. The night described exactly how my life was, dark and stormy. I passed the bridge I used to live under. Then I passed Dino's Bar 'n' Grill. The last stop was Dick's Music Store. They turned it into a small furniture shop. I stood there for a few minutes, staring at the front of the business. I was taking a small trip down memory lane in my head.

My clothes were drenched, and the picture I had was getting ruined. The alcohol was coursing through my veins, and I was starting to see double of everything. I turned around and faced toward the street. I closed my eyes and started praying. I whispered to myself, "Our Father, who art in heaven hallowed be thy name. Thy kingdom come, thy will be done. Give us this day our daily bread. And forgive us for our trespasses, as we forgive those who trespass against us. Lead us not into temptation, but deliver us from evil. For thine is the kingdom, the power and the glory, forever and ever."

I stepped off the curb, and with tires screeching, I heard the sound of a car horn getting louder. Headlights shining bright, I felt the impact of a car slamming into my hip. I saw the sky, then the ground and then the sky again. I slammed down hard on the pavement and slid about twenty feet from the headlights. I lay there on my back with my head facing toward the car. A lady got out of the driver's side and screamed, "Oh my god! Sir, are you OK?"

Once she realized I was unresponsive, she screamed again, "Someone dial 911, somebody, anybody, I need help!" The road was cold and wet, and blood was dripping out of my mouth. She came running up, kneeling down, and said frantically, "Hang in there, sir, I am going to get help."

My body was in a lot of pain. Another person pulled up and dialed 911. I couldn't see well, but I could hear it, "Yes, 911, please send an ambulance, there has been an accident involving a pedestrian. We are downtown right across from the old music store! Hurry please, he is bleeding badly!"

The lady driver said to me, "OK, hang in there, help is on the way." I could hear sirens in the distance as well as more people gathered around to pray for me. I saw the ambulance driver and passenger get out of the truck. They wheeled a stretcher in my direction. The headlights were so bright I could barely make out what all was going on. The rain continued to come down. I heard the EMT say, "He still has a pulse, I need the neck brace! Hang in there, buddy, you're going to be OK!"

They put the neck brace on and attempted to put me on the stretcher. I heard the EMT yell again, "We got to get him to the hospital quickly, he is bleeding internally!"

He said again, "I need you to breathe, sir, just breathe."

I tried to communicate back to him, but I couldn't. He said, "Don't talk, just breathe. OK, everyone please back away!" They got me on to the stretcher and put me in the back of the ambulance. One of the EMTs rode in the back with me to monitor my status. There was no way in hell I could move with the way they had me strapped down.

The hospital was only a couple miles away. I felt the ambulance stop and heard the back door open. I had my eyes closed the entire time and was just listening. It felt like I was starting to slip away. I heard nurses and doctors frantically yelling back and forth with each other. I could feel them wheeling me fast through the hallway. Facing the ceiling as each fluorescent fixture passed me by. The last thing I remembered hearing was a nurse say, "Oh, God, Doctor, we are losing him!"

"I need the defibrillator now!" the doctor yelled.

I tried to open my eyes, but everything was fading to black. This was it for me. I was dying. The road was coming to an end.

My breathing started slowing down, and then everything went quiet. The next thing I remember was lying in a hospital bed. I could hear the sound of the heart monitor beeping. An IV was stuck in my right arm. I felt a plastic tube across my face and stuffed into my nostrils. I was breathing better, and I was thinking I'm alive, and then I heard the door open and footsteps coming my way. I could barely move my head, so I couldn't see who it was. A curtain was extended all the way around my bed. I figured it was the doctor coming to tell me the news. The white curtain slowly opened. A calm, subtle voice spoke, "Hello, David." It was a very familiar voice. My vision was blurry, and my voice was weak, "Oh my god, John, is that you?"

"Yes, it's me John, stay still and try not to move. You're in a lot of pain, and your body is weak." He leaned in far enough over the bed that I could see him, and I started to smile.

I said, "I am so sorry you have to see me like this. My life has gone completely down the drain lately. This is the last place I thought I would ever see you."

"Yeah, I know, this isn't the place I was hoping to find you, but there is more you need to know."

"What do you mean? You're not making any sense."

"Sshh, just hear me out because there isn't much time," John said.

I was getting confused, "What do you mean, there isn't much time?" I asked.

John then went on to explain the most heartbreaking news that any man would want to hear. "You remember back in prison when I told you that I had a son?"

"Yeah, I remember, they took him away from you, did you find your son John?"

He paused for a second, and I saw tears filling his eyes.

"You, David, you were my son they took away from me." He reached out and grabbed my hand as I started to cry.

"No, it can't be, my parents died!" I cried.

"That was a lie they told you. You were so little, you don't remember. I have been wondering and worrying all my life about you. Wondering if there would ever come a day that I would be with my boy again. I've been following you ever since—" John stopped and started wiping his tears.

"Ever since what, John?"

Tears were flowing, and his lips were shaking as he said, "Ever since I died, son."

I cried and I cried and held his hand tighter.

"The cancer got to me about four months after your last visit with me. That's why I only have these few minutes to talk to you. I didn't find out until I passed on, and the man upstairs has given me this time to tell you everything. I am an angel, David."

I was choking as I was crying so hard. I was in purgatory, the passageway between heaven and hell. I cried out, "Please tell me it's my time to go, Dad."

"No, son, it's not your time just yet."

"Why! I have nothing left to live for. You're gone, and so is my baby girl. I am going to hell, ain't I?"

He said after wiping his tears, "Calm down and listen to me please. You have lived an incredible life, and your story is going to be told one day. You will be an inspiration to millions of people all over the world. You just have to hang in there, son, and don't ever try to kill yourself again. Emma and I won't be able to see you at all if that happens. She loves you with all her heart, and she will be OK. She told me to tell you that she loves you, and it's not your fault. Just know that I will be taking care of her, I promise. I love you very much, and I'm sorry. I wish I could change the past so I could give you a good life. I am glad that we got to spend the time we did together. I know it wasn't the best place in the world, but I am very proud of you. I wish I could have seen you grow up. I have to go now, son, and know that we will be watching over you." John let go of my hand and started to back up toward the door.

Tears were pouring down my face as I yelled, "Don't go, Dad, please! Please don't leave me!"

"Goodbye, son, I love you." He walked out the door, and I rolled out of the bed pulling the equipment down with me. I crawled to the door and cried out, "I love you, Dad! Oh, God, please take me!"

Then, out of nowhere, I felt a sharp pain running through my chest. I put my hand over my heart and screamed in pain. I curled up into a ball, and then I heard voices, "Doctor, we got a pulse! He is going to pull through!"

I was able to open my eyes. I looked around for a second and saw doctors and nurses standing everywhere. The doctor said to me, "Welcome back, David, we lost you there for a second."

I closed my eyes and passed out.

I eventually woke up again in a hospital bed. A nurse was standing in the corner of the room. I said to her in a weak voice, "What happened?"

The nurse said, "You stepped out in front of a car, and you almost didn't make it. They had to open you up to stop the bleeding. You lost a lot of blood, and your heart stopped, but thanks to our medical staff, you're going to be OK."

I was dressed in a hospital gown, and my body felt very weak. A TV was on just above the edge of the bed. The nurse walked over and said, "Here, David, take this medicine, it will help. You're going to feel funny for a couple of days, but that's normal. We will be keeping you here for a little bit to monitor your health. If there is anything you need, just hit the call button on your right." She walked out the door, and I leaned my head back into the pillow. I stared at the ceiling, and another tear came rolling down my face. I was thinking about what John just told me. He was my father this entire time. I failed at trying to kill myself, but after knowing there is an afterlife, I was never going to attempt that again. I now fully believed everything the Bible said. It was a life-changing moment.

Chapter 26

The Day That Never Comes

Ten years of my life went by, and April and I never spoke since the accident. I needed a fresh, new start in life, so I was living in Columbus and had my very own record store. It was called Taylor Records, and the inside was very long and narrow. Wooden crates held the records in alphabetical order. Only two aisles to walk down because I had display shelves extended down the middle of the store. On the far right and far left sides were more wooden crates full of records. Posters of my favorite bands were taped to the drop ceiling above. The counter was at the far end facing out so I could keep an eye on people entering my store. There was a small area in the back for storage. I did have two employees, Aaron Woodward and Billy

Morris, who worked for me part-time. Through the years, Amerex blew up with two multiplatinum-selling albums including the first record I recorded on. It bothered me for the longest time, but I was glad to see those guys become successful. I missed the days of practicing and gigging out, but I was starting to be happy again. I was still around music and helping kids was it for me.

On March 5th, 2010, I made a trip back to Sonic Lounge Studios to visit Joe Collins. When I arrived there, he had some band in there recording. I didn't want to be a jerk and interrupt, but as soon as I walked into the control room, I saw Joe sitting at the mixing board. He did a double take and said, "Oh my god, David, is that you?"

"Yeah, Joe, it's me."

He had some excitement in his voice as he said, "Good to see you, buddy. Wow, it has been a long time, hang on for a second." He hit the talk-back button and told the band in the room, "Hey, guys, take ten, and I will be right back." Then he stood up and said, "Please, David, have a seat and welcome back. Damn, it's been a long time since I've seen you. How's things going?"

I sat down on the couch and replied, "Oh, man, so much shit happened to me after we recorded that first album. My life has been a huge roller coaster ride." I was getting shook up as all the recording memories were coming back to me. I said, "I will try to sum it all up in a nutshell. Once the tour started, everything was going great. It was tough and very tiring, but we were managing just fine. We were three months into our tour when I got news that I never thought I would receive. I got word that my daughter was killed in a car wreck. Two cops showed up in Dallas to tell me the news. I had to leave the tour immediately. When I got back, I got word again that Amerex was replacing me."

"Oh my god, I didn't know all this," Joe blurted out.

I continued, "I couldn't cope with all of this, and I tried to kill myself by stepping in front of a car. Once I did that, I saw the light from above, and let me tell you, I will never try to do that again. So here I am, ten years later alive and well. Took a lot of time to heal.

Seeing the band become so successful and losing Emma took a toll on me. So I just went into hiding all these years."

Joe sat there like he saw a ghost and replied, "Oh my god, David, that is one hell of a story you just told me. I am very sorry to hear about your daughter. I have six kids, and I could only imagine what you went through. Don't let that band shit bother you anymore. If I were you, I would definitely write a book about this or something. If you need anything, you know I am here. You are more than welcome to stop in here anytime you want."

"Thanks, Joe, I do have a song I would like to record with you. It's called 'Forever Gone,' and I wrote it shortly after I got out of the hospital. It's about my family. I kinda shelved it for a while because the song has a lot of emotion to it, but I feel like I need to record it as soon as I can. I don't know why I haven't recorded earlier. Maybe because I was in too much pain. However, I am also going to be the one who sings it."

Joe replied, "Dude, absolutely, I'll tell you what, how about you come back in a couple days, and I will record it and master it for free?"

"Really, you would do that for me?" I said.

"Yes, a man like you has been through a lot, and so it would be my pleasure. So go home, relax, and get some sleep. I will see you in here tomorrow."

Joe had a good heart, and he cared about the musicians and the music they wrote. He said the best songs in the world come from the heart and the suffering that people have gone through. So I went home that night excited and thrilled to be back into the studio to record a song that meant so much to me. Joe recommended that I put new strings on right away to allow them to stretch in.

When the day rolled around, I packed up the acoustic and headed to the studio. Joe was there, and as I walked by the main room, he had it all set up for me. There was a wooden stool in the center of the room with a Shure Sm7 microphone hooked up. A DPA microphone was set up for the acoustic guitar. Joe was getting everything else set up in the control room as I gazed around. I walked in the control room with my guitar strapped to my back.

"What's up, Joe?"

"Hey, David, good to see you again. Just hang out for a second, while I get everything ready. I will need to set up your acoustic first. I have it set up out there for you to play and sing at the same time, if that's OK with you? I think it would be better for now to do a couple scratch takes, then track the acoustic, and then we can go and punch in the vocals afterward."

I agreed with him and pulled out the acoustic, so Joe could check the intonation to make sure it was holding the correct tone. In this process, he would adjust the truss rod in the neck of the guitar. It only took him about fifteen minutes, and then it was time to record the first take. I sat on the stool and checked the tuning one more time. I had headphones on so Joe could communicate with me. I could also see him through the glass window that looked into the control room. The song I wrote wasn't that difficult, only a two-chord progression in the verses and five chords in the chorus. I was playing the song in half a step down. I felt that it gave the acoustic sound a more dark emotional feel, and Joe agreed. Plus, it fit my vocal range better.

Joe hit the talk-back button and said to me, "OK, David, I am ready when you are, now remember this is just a scratch track, so don't worry if you mess up."

I took a deep breath and released it as I said, "OK, yeah, that's cool." I then started the opening strum and followed it up with the first verse. I sang, "I don't know what to say, when I heard the news today. Well, it seems to be that I lost a part of me. So I wrote this song today, just to ease my pain away. Now I don't know what to do, and I don't know where to go. I just wanted to let you know." I continued into the chorus as I sang, "I wish I could take back what I said. Don't want to be here anymore. Well, it hurts to see you go, and it tears me up inside! Can't take this anymore, just to see you lying there! Hurts to say goodbye! Please take this pain away!"

Tears started filling my eyes as I started the second verse, "As time starts to change, getting older every day, but the memory still remains. Of the good times that we had, I wanna start this over again. I want to hold you in my arms. Somebody make this go away, just give me one more chance." Then I would repeat the chorus again. After the second chorus, I did a small breakdown with vocals and repeated the chorus on out. Joe had the acoustic equalized just right, and it sounded so beautiful and relaxing. Like listening to the ocean waves on Laguna Beach.

After the first run-through of the song, Joe stood up from behind the mixing board and hit the talk-back button. He said, "Dude, I changed my mind. That was a beautiful take, and I can feel the emotion and intensity from you, so I think it would better to track the main vocals and guitar while you're in there. Everything sounds amazing in here and having you strum along and singing just feels right instead of tracking everything individually. We will punch in the harmonies later, plus I have a killer idea with an electric guitar part. So let's do three or four takes because you are killing it in there."

I just nodded my head the entire time. Joe was the pro, and if he says it sounds amazing, then he is correct. It only took four takes, and the main vocals and guitar were complete. After that, Joe picked up his Thunderbird and said, "Now I am going to add a little bass."

Many people don't realize how important bass really is. The only way I could get dumb people to understand this is when you're in the car, just turn your bass knob all the way off during your favorite song. Then turn it up halfway into the middle of the song, and then it will hit them. Joe laid down a simple bass line, and that made a world of difference. Once that step was done, it was time for his electric-guitar idea to come to life. He used a Fender telecaster with a slight tremolo effect, and that became a beautiful addition to the song. It felt like David Gilmour from Pink Floyd was playing in the distance. The last thing to do was punch in the harmonies on the choruses. When the song was finally finished, I felt like I could put the past behind me and move on with my life. I was able to take all the sadness and emotion and put it into that song. That is the beauty of music, and a lot of people forget that. I could lay my head down at night and know that my family would be proud of me. Shortly after I recorded the song, I went back to living my life.

Three days later, I was just about to close down the store when one of my employees named Billy came into the back and said, "Hey, David, there is a man here to see you, he looks very familiar."

"OK, I will be out in a second." I had to wrap up a few minor things in the back, and then I went out front. I said to Billy, "Where is he?"

"Standing in the corner looking at some records." I walked over and approached a man from behind. He had short hair while wearing a leather jacket and a pair of rugged blue jeans. I said to the man's back, "Hello, sir, can I help you?"

The man didn't turn around at first. He continued flipping through the records and replied, "It's good to hear your voice, David."

"Do I know you, sir?"

He turned around slowly and said, "I believe you do."

Once he turned, there stood Sebastian Rose. I barely recognized him with the short hair. There was an awkward moment of silence, and then I said, "I thought you would be the last person I would ever see again."

"Yeah, I was thinking the same. I would like to have a word with you in private if that's OK? I know it's been a long time, and you're probably still upset, but I really would like to talk to you."

"You got some balls showing up here, but give me second, I got to send my employees home, and then we can talk." I told Billy and Aaron to go clock out and go home. I flipped the sign on the glass door from Open to Closed.

We stood in the middle of the store and had our much-needed conversation. I said, "So what the hell brings you to my store? I figured since you were a big rock star, you wouldn't ever speak to me again."

Sebastian explained, "I know it's been over ten years since we talked, and I know you probably have a lot of hate built up, but just hear me out. The band life has completely consumed our lives, and I just want to say I am sorry for not being there for you when you lost your little girl. I couldn't imagine what that must have been like. Staying out of touch was an asshole move, and I'm sorry, David. I also found out about your attempted suicide as well. The guys and

I were thinking about you the other week and how much we miss you. You were a big part of our lives, and the damn record label has had us by the balls. They pretty much controlled our music career for the past ten years. Including the music on our second, third, and fourth album. They made us replace you with Cameron. We made a dumb decision signing that contract, but I guess we can't complain too much because the money and fame was good."

I interrupted and said, "Money and fame isn't everything, you should know that, plus you have no idea what I went through. Almost every day, I would hear you on the radio. Every time you had a show nearby, that's all I would hear about. Amerex this, Amerex that. I want you to know that I'm over it now and moved on with my life, especially after my near-death experience. So why are you here, Sebastian? What made you come back?"

"David, I'm sorry, I really am, but we got something big coming up, and I want to ask you if you will be a part of it. It's something that David Taylor needs to be a part of because it wouldn't be right."

My first intention was that he wanted me to come back to the band, but what came out of his mouth took me by surprise. He said, "Jesus, David, you have lived one hell of a life so far. You went from prison to a musician to a father. I became an asshole, OK? The money and fame got to us. I'm sorry for forgetting who my friend really was, not just a friend, but a brother who I wish I had back in my life. I was thinking the other day that nothing would make me happier than to have you join us on stage in front of 90,000 people. It's by far the biggest shows we are headlining, and I want you to join us on stage and tell your rock 'n' roll story to all those people."

I put my head down for a second and then lifted my head up with tears filling my eyes and said, "There is only one arena that I know of that we used to talk about it when we started playing. Dreaming one day we would get to play there."

Sebastian was nodding his head up and down, and then I said, "Wembley Stadium in London, England?" Sebastian said, "Yes, David, you are correct. The dream has come true for us, and so please join us."

I tried not to act like I was excited, but after hearing this, all I could think about is what my father told me the night of my accident. He said that this day would eventually come. This was a chance for me to finally experience the dream. I was thinking in my head what my family would want, and so I told Sebastian, "I'm in, how are Marc and Anthony doing?"

"Well, they had some drug problems for a while, and that damn near destroyed all of us. It was tough trying to keep the band together. We would fight constantly over creative direction, but we would always make up and never forget why we started this. We have all been sober for a couple years now and still going strong. I want you to know that the rest of the guys don't know that you will be there. It's a total surprise to them as well."

"Don't they know where you're at now? I thought you're in the middle of a tour now?" I asked.

"We are on a tour break, and I used all my time and connections to track you down before I go back on. Trust me, they will be stoked to see you."

"What about your other guitar player Cameron? Will he be pissed off at me?"

"Oh, he will be fine, now that we are out of our record contract with Unique, we can call the shots," he said.

I stuck my hand out to shake his, but he looked at me and quoted a line from the movie *Tommy Boy*, "Brothers don't shake hands, brothers got to hug." He gave me a big hug as we burst out laughing. It felt good to see Sebastian after all these years. It was best to let bygones be bygones. Then he said to me, "OK, the show is a month from now. I will be in touch, and I'll go ahead and get your plane ticket and have everything else set up for you including a ride and a hotel. I will see you in London, my brother."

I stopped him one more time before he headed out the door. "Do I need to bring anything in particular?" I asked.

"Just your passport and you, my friend," he answered.

CHAPTER 27

Nothing Else Matters

When I arrived in London, I was completely blown away at how pretty England looked from the sky. It was a very long flight over the ocean. Took over seven hours to arrive. One of my biggest fears was flying over the ocean. I tried my best to sleep through most of the flight. Once I landed at the airport, they had a long black limo waiting outside to escort me to the hotel. This limo looked like what you would see pull up at the red carpet. Sebastian booked me a very nice suite that had an amazing view of the stadium. Once I checked into the room, I stared out the window and was amazed that I was only a few hours away from playing the biggest show of my life. With my reflection in the window, I closed my eyes and took a deep breath. The butterflies in my stomach were about to burst out of me. I ordered a nice steak dinner around 4:00 PM, compliments of the hotel.

Sebastian wasn't really clear on all the instructions on what I will be doing once I got there, so I had to play it by ear. Five thirty rolls around, and my limo driver came knocking saying it was time to head out. The rest of the guys must have already arrived at Wembley. I left the hotel and headed toward the stadium. When I got closer, I saw a billboard saying "Amerex Live Tonight at Wembley Stadium." The closer I got, I saw people walking to the stadium wearing Amerex merchandise. They were jumping around and hollering out loud. They were ready for the show.

We pulled up to a gate, and a security guard let us in. There were over twenty-five semitrucks parked out back. He pulled up to one of the back entrances and dropped me off. The driver said to me, "Go through that door, and there will be a man waiting for you on the other side. Good luck, David."

I stepped out fully dressed and ready to go. I was wearing a badass pair of jeans along with a brand new pair of Chuck Taylor. I was also wearing a black leather jacket with shiny silver buttons. I could hear screams coming from inside the stadium. The sound system was rattling the entire place. I approached the back door and went in. On the other side of the door was a man leaning against the hallway smoking a cigarette. One man I didn't expect to see. I said, "Waylon, is that you?"

He had a big smile, "Yes, it is, good to see you, David. The boys invited me out, and I wouldn't have missed it for the world. Sebastian said tonight was a special night, and I'm so glad to see you will be a part of it." He gave me a big hug, and I replied, "Damn, it's good to see you, friend. I wasn't expecting to see you out here. You look great, man."

"Yes, same here, Sebastian set it all up, so follow me. We don't have much time." I followed Waylon down the concrete hallway to the back of the stage. The closer I got, the louder the music was getting. I could hear those boys up there giving it everything they got. There were all kinds of equipment cases everywhere plus a shitload of roadies and stage crew workers walking around. Waylon handed me my backstage pass and yelled, "OK, wait here! I don't know when exactly you will go up, but Sebastian will call your name. The stage manager just notified him that you are here, so it's only a matter of minutes!" We had to yell at each other because the music was so loud.

I yelled back, "Dude, I am so nervous right now, I'm about to shit myself!"

"Don't worry, you will be fine! Just head up the ramp once he calls for you. I am going to finish watching the show now! Good luck!"

"That's it! All I have to do is wait here?" I said out loud.

"Yeah, that's all I was instructed to do. Give them hell, David!"

The stage was so massive, and all I could see was the back of Marc's head as he sat on this huge drum riser. His drums were so shiny, the reflection on the lights would almost blind you. I could see fire and CO2 exploding. Everything we talked about when it came to stage presence was happening here tonight. Then I heard the guys end their current song. The crowd roared, and they roared. The roars were almost as loud as the sound system.

Once the crowd calmed down, I heard Sebastian step up to the mic and said, "Ladies and gentlemen, tonight is a special night. And what makes this night so special is that we have a special guest here with us tonight. Ten years ago, I started this band in my house with a friend of mine. That man was a very talented guitar player. After recording our first demo, we landed our first record deal. You all remember that album *Turn Up the Heat*!"

The crowd screamed and hollered louder. Sebastian went on, "Many of you don't know, but we did a six-month tour following the release of that album. When we were three months in, he disappeared off the tour. Come to find out he had a very tragic moment happen in his life, and we had no other choice but to replace him."

The crowd starting booing, and he continued, "I know, people, I know, but there is more to this story, however. Ten years later, I was able to track him down, ladies and gentlemen! Please welcome back the man who helped this band all the way back from day one! Make some noise for our long-lost brother, David Taylor!" I started to walk up the ramp and out on to the stage. Hundreds of lights shining down on the stage and a massive line array speaker system was hanging from each side of the stage. This is what being a rock star was all about. There was a sea of people watching and cheering. Thousands upon thousands of people were in attendance tonight.

Marc and Anthony almost started crying. Anthony walked over with his bass and gave me a hug. He said to me, "Holy crap, dude, I wasn't expecting this. Sebastian mentioned something about a surprise, and I am blown away. I missed you, man."

"I missed you too, Anthony, you look great, dude."

Marc stood up from behind his kit and gave me a hug as well. He whispered in my ear, "I wasn't expecting this, but I never thought I would see you again. We were just talking about you the other day, and I am so fucking glad to see you."

I said, "Damn it, dude, you're going to make me cry in front of all these people." I turned back to the front of the stage, and all I could see was a sea of people with their hands up and yelling. I couldn't hold it, so I started crying. It was that emotional. I raised my hand and waved at them. They cheered and they cheered as I stepped up to the mic and said, "Thank you! Thank you, guys, so much. It feels so good to be here. I never thought this day would come. I never thought I would be standing on a stage in front of all of you. I am very proud of these guys and their success." I looked over at them and then burst into tears as I said, "I fucking love you, guys."

The crowd went even crazier and cheered even louder. Once the crowd calmed down, Sebastian stepped back to the mic and said, "We love you too, brother, and that's why I promised you could share your story to these people. However, David, I think it would be better if you told your story through this!"

I looked over, and Cameron, their guitar player, came out from behind the stage with Sebastian's old Gibson Les Paul I used to play. Cameron walked up to me, handed me the guitar, and said, "Tell your story through this, my friend. It's an honor to meet you, and I've heard great things about you." Cameron put that Gibson around my neck and then I turned back toward the crowd. Something caught my attention up in the rafters of the stadium, and so I looked up. On the catwalk, I saw John holding Emma's hand, and they both were waving at me. Emma was standing there smiling with her little pink princess outfit, and I'm pretty sure she was mouthing the words "Love you, Daddy." I put my right hand up and waved back at them. A teardrop streamed down my face as Sebastian walked up to me and said, "You, OK?"

I turned to Sebastian and put my left hand on his shoulder and said with confidence, "Yeah, everything's just fine." I looked back up, and they were gone. I raised my fist high to the sky; 90,000 people raised their fists with me as I glanced over at the three of them. Anthony, Marc, and Sebastian all had huge smiles on their faces. Once again, we were reunited and shared the love for music just like we did when we first started.

David Taylor passed away that night in his hotel room. There was no evidence of any narcotics or foul play involved with his death. The only thing that was found next to him was his journal he began when he was in prison. David became a musical inspiration to millions of people all over the world. His death remains a mystery to this day, but millions of people believed that once his story was told, it was time for him to be reunited with his family. If you would like to listen to David's song, "Forever Gone," please scan the QR code below with your smartphone or tablet.

AUTHOR'S NOTE

I want to thank you all for taking the time to read my first novel. I personally want to thank my family and my old bandmates for being a huge part of my life. My life experiences with you over the years have helped inspire me to write this novel. I know we have been through a lot during our music career, but I wouldn't change it for the world. I would also like to thank producer Joe Viers and Nashville performing artist John Carroll for recording my song "Forever Gone" which David wrote in the novel. You two brought the song to life, and I couldn't have done it without your help. God bless you for your hard work.

Thank you Jeff

Best Wishes

ABOUT THE AUTHOR

Anthony Dunn grew up in Lancaster, Ohio, and learned how to play guitar at age fifteen. He began studying audio/video production just after high school. After two years of college, he formed a rock band called Cross Solder with a fellow high school friend. They went on to record two albums and produce three music videos. Following their dreams, he began to struggle with life inside and outside the band. After six years of performing, the group disbanded and which inspired him to write his first novel called *The Dreamer and the Believer*. Anthony currently lives in Ohio with his fiancé and two daughters.

CPSIA information can be obtained
at www.ICGtesting.com
Printed in the USA
FFOW03n1544151017
41047FF